"What if I said I wanted you to kiss me?" Scarlet asked.

Mason squeezed his eyelids tightly shut to block out the image of her looking up at him with those full lips and sad eyes. It was as though she could sense his weakness and knew that she was it.

The hand on his chest lifted, but before Mason could open his eyes, he felt her palm against his cheek. She softly caressed his face, letting her thumb drag across his bottom lip. "Aren't you going to say anything?"

"It's not what I want to say, Scarlet—it's what I want to do."

She moved closer to him, pressing her firm breasts against his chest. Her whole body was aligned with his, reminding him of how she was the perfect fit for him in so many ways.

"What do you want to do, Mason?"

He couldn't hold back any longer. His eyes flew open to look down at her before the floodgates gave way. "This," he said.

Diving forward, he scooped her face into his hands and pulled her mouth to his.

The Baby Favour

ANDREA LAURENCE

First published in Great Britain 2017
By Mills & Boon, an imprint of HarperCollins*Publishers*
1 London Bridge Street, London, SE1 9GF

Large Print edition 2017

© 2017 Andrea Laurence

ISBN: 978-0-263-07213-6

Our policy is to use papers that are natural, renewable and recyclable products and made from wood grown in sustainable forests. The logging and manufacturing processes conform to the legal environmental regulations of the country of origin.

Printed and bound in Great Britain
by CPI Antony Rowe, Chippenham, Wiltshire

Andrea Laurence is an award-winning author of contemporary romances filled with seduction and sass. She has been a lover of reading and writing stories since she was young. A dedicated West Coast girl transplanted into the Deep South, she is thrilled to share her special blend of sensuality and dry, sarcastic humor with readers.

To Adoptive & Foster Parents Everywhere—

Whatever your reason for opening your hearts and your homes to a child in need, thank you.

One

As a general rule, phone calls that came after midnight were bad news.

An hour ago, when Scarlet Spencer had looked at her caller ID and seen her estranged husband's name, a moment of excitement had rushed through her. The other kind of calls that came at this hour were emotional outpourings brought on by late nights and alcohol. She'd hoped that it was the latter—that perhaps he'd changed his mind about the divorce—but she was to be disappointed. Now she was walking through the front door of Cedars-Sinai Medical Center in Los Angeles just after two in the morning and she didn't know why.

All she knew was that Mason had called and asked her to come. Despite everything that was happening between them, she knew she had to do as he asked. There was something in his voice that scared her. Mason had been her rock for the last nine years. Through the ups and downs of their marriage, he had been the one to hold her hand. She got the feeling that tonight, she was returning the favor.

As she walked through the doors of the hospital, she tried to brace herself for seeing Mason again. She hadn't seen him since he moved out two months ago and she didn't know how it would feel. After nine years together, he wasn't hers anymore. He wasn't hers to hold or care for. She would have to remind herself of that as she consoled him tonight.

Before she reached the elevators, she found Mason sitting on a bench in the hallway. The first time they'd met, she'd instantly been enchanted by the beautiful surfer boy with his golden skin, eyes as blue as the sea and messy brown hair. When he smiled, his dimples had melted her insides. Just a glimpse of him now was enough to set her heart racing in her chest even all these years later.

Tonight, however, there were no smiles. He was slumped in his seat, holding his head in his hands.

He looked defeated. Scarlet had seen that in him only a few times in all these years. Most of the time, he was the confident, successful CEO of Spencer Surf Shops. The guy who never failed at anything. Who always knew the right decision to make. Sexy, bold and sure of himself. Rarely did that facade crack. Once, when he found out he couldn't give her a child. The second time, when he couldn't keep the judge from giving their adopted son back to his biological mother. The third time was when he walked out the door, leaving her and their marriage behind.

She couldn't imagine what happened tonight that could bring that look of despair back to his face. "Mason?" she asked as she approached.

Her husband shot up in his seat, turning to her with eyes more red than blue. He stood quickly, his jaw flexed tight as he tried to hold everything in. He didn't speak right away, as though if he opened his mouth, a torrent of emotions would pour out of him instead.

"What's happened? Is it Jay?"

Scarlet knew that Mason's younger brother, Jay, had been battling stage four melanoma for several months. The last she'd heard, they'd gotten the devastating news that the cancer had spread into all his major organs and they were discontinuing treatment. It wouldn't surprise her to find out that Jay had finally lost his battle. Something about the look on Mason's face, however, made her worry that this was something much worse.

"No," Mason said at last. "It's Rachel."

"Jay's wife?" Scarlet felt her chest tighten. Her sister-in-law had been like a true sister to her. As an only child, Scarlet had enjoyed having Rachel around to talk to and share marriage war stories with. The idea of Rachel raising their daughter alone after Jay passed had weighed heavily on her mind since she found out the news. Luna was only a year old and would never remember her father. "What happened?"

"She's dead."

Scarlet could only clap her hand over her mouth to hold in the painful gasp. It couldn't be true. The universe wasn't that cruel. Baby Luna was already losing her father. To lose her mother, too… "How…?" She couldn't get the words out. How could something like this happen?

"It was a freak accident. She fell down the stairs carrying a basket of laundry. I can imagine her mind has been all over the place dealing with Jay's illness. She fell in just the right way to break her neck instantaneously. Their housekeeper found her."

Scarlet didn't know what to say. Of everything that had run through her head since she received the call, Rachel's death was the last thing she expected. It was so bitterly tragic on its own, not to mention when it was compounded by Jay's illness. "Does Jay know?" she whispered through her fingers.

Mason nodded. "He's the one who called and told me about it."

She could only squeeze her eyes shut and shake her head. This wasn't the way things were supposed to happen. Her own life was a mess and she was dealing with that, but Jay and Rachel... Her heart just ached. Tears welled beneath her eyelids. A moment later, she felt Mason's arms wrap around her and she didn't fight it. Instead, she melted into him and let her tears wet the front of his dress shirt. She tried not to think about how good it felt to be in his arms again. How much she missed his scent in her lungs and his warmth surrounding her. He was just comforting her, perhaps comforting himself, and nothing more.

That thought was able to cut through the grief,

stab her in her tender underbelly and remind her to keep her emotional distance. With a soft sniffle, she pulled away from him and took a step back. When her gaze met Mason's, there was a flash of pain there unrelated to the accident. It was as though he was hurt she'd pulled away so soon. As much as she might like to stay in his arms all night, that wouldn't help her get over him. It was hard enough being in the same room with him knowing he didn't want her anymore.

Despite everything, Scarlet couldn't help but wonder why he'd called her tonight. They were getting a divorce and had hardly been speaking for the last two months after he'd moved out of their Malibu beach house. He had family in town. Friends. Surely there was someone else he would want here with him instead of her. He was the one who walked away, after all. Away from her, away from their life together...

Mason cleared his throat and wiped his eyes. "I'm sorry to drag you down here in the middle of the night, but Jay asked to see us."

Scarlet frowned. "Us?"

He nodded. "He's waiting on us to come up. He's on the oncology floor."

Mason turned toward the elevator, not giving Scarlet a chance to argue with him, as usual. She followed him, both of them silent until they exited on the third floor. Halfway down the hallway, they entered a room with the name J. Spencer written on the whiteboard.

Scarlet held her breath as she stepped inside. She hadn't seen Jay in a while and she was worried about how she'd react to seeing him in such rough shape. At first, a privacy curtain blocked all but his blanketed legs, then Mason pushed it aside.

The man lying in the bed was half of the robust brother-in-law she'd once known. He'd easily lost fifty pounds on a tall frame that needed every bit of it. His thick brown hair, so much like Mason's, had thinned. His skin was sallow. But the Jay she knew was still in there somewhere—the life of the party, the comic relief, the easygoing counterpoint to Mason's perfectionism.

"Hey there," Jay said in a raspy voice as he spied Scarlet slipping into the room. She reached out and took his extended hand as he offered it to her. "You're looking beautiful as always, sister."

Scarlet bit at her bottom lip to keep from crying. "I won't be able to keep it up if you continue to interrupt my beauty sleep," she quipped. Jay preferred to keep things light even in the darkest moments, so she'd do her best to comply.

"I know." Jay's gaze grew distant as he stared off for a moment. "It couldn't be avoided. Did Mason tell you what happened?"

Scarlet could only nod as she slipped down into the chair beside the bed. "I'm so sorry, Jay."

Jay shook his head. "Don't worry about me. I won't be wasting away without her. She and I will have a happy reunion before too long. But I asked you both here because I'm worried about what's going to happen to Luna."

Scarlet felt stupid. She'd focused on the trauma

of the loss and hadn't even considered the fact that Luna would be orphaned soon. No wonder Jay was up in the middle of the night worried about his daughter's future.

"We want you to raise her. The paperwork officially just names Mason as her guardian for some reason our lawyers explained but I never understood, but of course we intended to leave her to both of you. I know how badly you both wanted a child. This isn't the way I expected it to happen, but I hope that you're open to the possibility of adopting Luna and raising her as your own."

"She'll always be your child, Jay," Mason said.

Jay shook his head. "She won't remember us, Mason. You and Scarlet will be the mother and father she knows and I'm okay with that. When she's older, you can tell her about us and about how much we adored her. But I hope you'll embrace this opportunity and raise her with all the love and support that Rachel and I would've given her."

Scarlet's heart lodged in her throat as she realized the implications of Jay's words. She couldn't make a sound, she could only sit stunned and listen to the two brothers discuss her life like nothing had changed between them. Mason hadn't told his brother they were getting a divorce yet. Jay was speaking about their future as though he expected them to raise his daughter together. What were they going to do?

Mason reached out and took Scarlet's hand, squeezing it tightly to silence her concerns. Her gaze met his for a moment and she knew that he sensed her panic. "Of course we will," he said.

"Promise me," Jay said.

Mason swallowed hard, squeezing his eyes shut before nodding. "I promise, Jay. Luna will want for nothing. She will have all the love that we can give her."

Jay finally seemed pleased. He relaxed back into his bed and took a deep, labored breath. "Thank you. You know, when you write your will, you never imagine you'll actually need it. At least you hope you won't. In the morning, I'll have my attorneys start the process of having you declared her legal and physical guardian, Mason. I can't fill that role from my hospital bed, and before long, you'll be all she has anyway. Once I'm gone, I hope the two of you will consider adopting her."

"Of course," Mason said. His grip on her grew ever tighter as Jay spoke. "You don't need to worry about a thing."

"You haven't told your brother that we're getting a divorce?"

Mason halted his quick pace. They were just exiting the hospital and heading toward their cars when she finally confronted him. He was thankful she'd waited that long so no one could overhear the truth he desperately wanted to keep from his brother. He pivoted on the asphalt and turned to look at his soon-to-be ex-wife.

He'd tried not to react to seeing her again for the first time since he moved out, but not even his grief could suppress his response to Scarlet.

Even now, after spending the last hour with her under the worst possible circumstances, his heart still skipped a beat when their eyes met. There was an undeniable connection between them that time and distance hadn't dulled. He didn't know if anything could.

She was the most beautiful women he'd ever seen in person, and LA was filled with beautiful people. In his eyes, no one could compare. Scarlet had long brown curls that trailed down her back, soft brown eyes and a disarming smile that had immediately caught his attention when they met. That was just the beginning of her appeal, he soon learned. She was also talented, smart, sensitive and a wonderful mother. At least for the short period of time she had been able to be one.

"No, I haven't told him. I didn't tell anyone in my family about the divorce yet."

"Why?"

"Why?" Mason repeated, running his fingers anxiously through his hair. "Because my brother has spent the last few months of his life battling terminal cancer. My parents are a wreck, barely holding it together. I didn't want to dump more on them. And really, the demise of our marriage seems fairly inconsequential in comparison, don't you think? They've been too caught up to even notice they haven't seen you in weeks."

"Of course it doesn't compare, but it's hardly insignificant. Now, because you haven't told anyone, Jay thinks we're going to raise Luna as one big, happy family." Scarlet's large brown eyes reflected the panic that he'd felt the moment he realized what Rachel's death would mean for him.

"I know," he admitted. "But how could I possibly tell a man in his position no?" He remembered his brother asking about putting him in the will not long after Luna was born. He'd agreed. Of course he'd take his niece in an emergency. He just never expected there to be an actual emergency. Or if there was, that it would happen at the worst possible time in his own life.

His lawyer had just sent him a draft of the mediated divorce settlement to review. Once they agreed on terms, it was a matter of signing off and filing it with the judge. Mason had moved out of the house he and Scarlet had bought together in Malibu and got a place in the Hollywood Hills. The new place was definitely a bachelor pad, not a single-dad pad. It was a midcentury modern design decorated with lots of glass, wood and chrome, completely unsuitable for an infant just starting to walk.

Then again, the home he'd shared with Scarlet in Malibu would be perfect. It still had a decorated nursery in it. She'd shut the room up and left it as it was the day they took their adopted son, Evan, back to his birth mother. The home also had an open floor plan with soft, safe surfaces that were fully baby proofed over a year ago.

It also had Scarlet, the mother that Luna would desperately need. That was where Luna should be. Mason was happy to have children with Scarlet when she wanted them, but the idea of being a single father to his niece was horrifying. He didn't know anything about babies, and he was certain Jay wouldn't leave Luna to him if he knew Scarlet was out of the picture.

The trick was convincing her to go along with this. After their adoption plans went south, she swore she would never go through that again. Was asking her to take in Luna, even temporarily, going to aggravate the wound? He didn't know. All he did know was that he'd made a promise to his brother and he would do whatever he had to to keep his word.

"I know that I have no reason to ask you for anything and you have no reason to go along with it. But you were there in Jay's hospital room, Scarlet. You heard him beg me—*us*—to take care of Luna. He was worried enough about leaving Rachel all alone, and now he's powerless to do anything but leave his daughter behind. I know our situation is complicated, but I couldn't tell him no. I need your help."

Scarlet crossed her arms over her chest. He knew from years together that it was her defensive posture. She was uncomfortable with this entire situation. "What are you asking of me, Mason? Do you want us to get back together just so you don't have to do this alone?"

"No, of course not." But what *did* he want? He really hadn't had enough time to process what all this would mean. Life-changing moments that arrived in the wee hours of the morning were hard to work through with a combination of stress and sleep deprivation. He couldn't process a long-term plan at this point; he could only focus on his next steps. The most important things were to make sure Luna was safe and Jay was at ease.

"For now, I just need you to do me two favors. First, please let's keep the divorce a secret from Jay and the rest of my family until after…" Mason couldn't finish the sentence. He still hadn't fully accepted the fact that his brother had only weeks left to live. Skin cancer was supposed to involve removing a bad mole and getting a lecture about sunscreen. It wasn't supposed to strike down an otherwise healthy father in his early thirties.

Scarlet watched him silently with dark eyes that didn't betray what she was thinking. She was always too hard for him to read. Whatever happened inside Scarlet's head was a secret from Mason. To this day, he wasn't sure if she blamed him for the fact that they couldn't have children. It was his fault, really, but did she look at him and see a barren future because of him? He didn't know. He also didn't know if she felt he was responsible for everything that happened with Evan. Had he fought hard enough to keep him? Had he hired all the best attorneys their money could buy to keep their son in their home? He thought he had, but it hadn't been enough.

All he knew was how he felt, and he felt like a failure where Scarlet was concerned. Mason wasn't the kind of man who failed at anything. He turned a small Venice Beach surf store he started in college into a chain with locations at every major beach in California, Florida and Hawaii. Spencer Surf Shops was more successful than he'd ever dreamed. But none of that mattered to him when he saw the brokenhearted look on Scarlet's face the day they took Evan away. He had failed her in the one dream she longed to fulfill more than any other.

"Okay. What's the second favor?" she asked at last.

"I need to move back into the house." He held up his hand to stop her inevitable protest. "Not forever. I don't want you to think I'm just trying to sweet-talk you into taking me back so I have a permanent babysitter. But I want to create the illusion of a secure future for Luna with the two of us to give Jay some peace of mind. Everyone thinks we're still together."

Scarlet flinched. "You walked out on me and now you just expect me to let you move back in?"

Mason tried not to let her reaction hurt his feelings. He was the one who had left, although he didn't like the idea that she'd already gotten used to living without him. They were together nine years. "Yes, that's what I'm asking, but you know I wouldn't if I had any other choice. It's just for however much time Jay has left. It will also give me some time to get my place ready for a baby. Our house has a nursery ready to go."

Scarlet's already pale skin seemed to blanch at his words. "Evan's nursery? You want to put Luna in Evan's room?"

Mason's jaw tightened. Scarlet's protection of Evan's space was something that he'd never challenged before. He knew it wasn't healthy to keep the room like a shrine to a child who was never returning, but pushing the issue with her seemed like a cruel fight to pick.

"It's an unused nursery," Mason clarified. Evan was never going to use it ever again. It was just a room with a crib, a changing table, and some baby supplies and toys that would help ease the situation they were in. "I'm not saying Luna has to stay there forever."

Scarlet's lips flattened into a tight line of displeasure, but she didn't argue with him. Instead, she seemed to be considering his request for a moment, finally dropping her arms at her sides.

"Okay, fine. You can stay at the house and bring Luna. But," she emphasized, "I'm not going to be your nanny, Mason. I've got a new gallery opening in San Francisco in two weeks, not to mention a large commissioned piece for a hotel in Maui. I'm behind on it because of everything that's happened between us and I have to get it done."

"That's fair," Mason said cautiously. "What do you need to make this work for us?"

"I'm happy to keep up appearances for Jay's sake, but you need to get a nanny to take care of Luna. I won't—no, I can't—go into Evan's room. I don't even like the idea of Luna using it, but I know that's unreasonable. You can use it, but don't expect me to be in there singing lullabies and rocking Luna to sleep. Please don't ask me to."

Mason watched as frustrated, glassy tears formed in Scarlet's eyes. It had been over a year since the judge awarded Evan back to his biological mother, but it may as well have been yester-day as far as Scarlet was concerned.

He had hoped that she might enjoy the time with her niece, but that didn't appear to be the case. She actually seemed repelled by the idea, which surprised him, but he wouldn't push the issue. If she agreed to the two favors that really mattered, he would find a way to make it work even if Scarlet was hands-off with Luna.

"I understand. Thank you for doing this. I'll see about a nanny first thing in the morning."

"Where is the baby now?" she asked.

"With my parents." It gave them something to focus on other than the grief. Luna was the same happy baby she always was. For her, noth-ing was different and that was a good distraction for them. "They'll probably keep her until Ra-chel's memorial service."

Scarlet nodded and reached into her purse. She pulled out a key and handed it to him. "This is to the house. I had the locks changed after you moved out. Just let me know you're on your way before you show up. Remember this isn't your place anymore."

Without another word, Scarlet turned and headed toward her car in the hospital parking lot. Mason watched her drive away with an aching feeling of disappointment in his stomach. He hadn't been able to shake that feeling the last few years of their marriage as they battled to start a family. He'd hoped that maybe when they were apart, the feeling would go away. It only got worse.

Scarlet had agreed to do him these favors, but he could tell she didn't want to. She had loved her little niece, but she resisted the idea of being hands-on with her. He hadn't had time to ponder the possibilities of what Luna could mean for their relationship, but it was clear that those ideas would just be fantasies. She didn't want anything to do with Luna. She wanted a child of her own. Once they were divorced, there was no reason for her to even pretend to be a family. Hell, that was why he'd left in the first place, so she wouldn't be held back from her dream.

That meant that once Jay passed away, Mason was going to be raising his niece all on his own.

A feeling of overwhelming panic started to wash over him. It felt like the first time he'd caught a huge wave surfing and had been engulfed by the harsh cone of water. He could only brace himself for the inevitable wipeout, knowing he was in way over his head.

Two

"You just need to go in there. Get it over with."

Scarlet turned to her manager, April, with a frown. They were sitting on her poolside deck overlooking the Pacific Ocean. "All right, you're cut off. No more wine for you." She picked up the bottle of chardonnay from the table and moved it out of her friend and employee's reach.

"I'm not drunk. I'm serious, Scarlet. Do it right now. I'll even go with you. Just open the door and step into the nursery. I think once you do it you'll feel better. It's just a room. It doesn't have any power over you that you don't give it."

"Thank you, Dr. Phil. I'll take that under consideration, but I'm not going in there right now." April was Scarlet's best friend, but she was regretting confiding in her about her latest situation with Mason. She was from the school of tough love and wouldn't pull any punches if she thought Scarlet needed to hear the truth.

"Does anyone go in there? Ever?"

"The housekeeper goes in to clean once a week."

"Did Mason ever go in there?"

Scarlet hesitated to answer, the memories of that night flooding through her mind like it was yesterday. "He did once. The night they took Evan away. He sat on the floor and cried. Losing Evan was hard on us both. Adopting that beautiful baby boy was a dream come true for us after struggling so long with infertility and sitting on the waiting list to get a baby. It was the best four months of my life. And then when the mother changed her mind…"

April reached across the table and took Scarlet's hand. "I know it was hard on you. And I'm not going to be the jerk who tells you to move on and forget about him, because that's never going to happen. You loved that little boy more than anything. Hell, I couldn't get you to put him down long enough to paint. But I do think that you're being unreasonable about the nursery. It's just a room filled with furniture like any other room. Once Mason and Luna move out, maybe you need to redecorate."

Scarlet snatched her hand away. "Redecorate?"

"Yes. Donate the furniture and baby clothes to a needy family. Paint the walls. Maybe turn it into an office or a yoga studio. Something that won't haunt you every day about what you lost."

Scarlet took a large sip of wine and sat back in her Adirondack chair. April was right. She knew she was right. She just hadn't been able to make herself do it. In her heart, it was Evan's room. It was their chance at a baby, as brief as it was, and changing that room meant that she was giving up on that part of her life. Or at least it felt that way.

"After they move out, I'll consider it," she agreed reluctantly. That answer would hopefully be enough to appease April, but not require her to march into the house and do something about it right that instant.

April gave her a satisfied smile and took a bite of the homemade guacamole and chips she'd brought with her for their girls' night in. "When is Mason moving in?"

"The funeral service for Rachel is tomorrow, so probably tomorrow night or the next morning."

"Are you prepared for having your soon-to-be ex-husband living in the house again?"

Scarlet sighed. She wasn't really sure how she felt about it. "It's hard to say. This whole situation is so complicated. On one hand, he hasn't been gone that long, so having him back in the house may just feel like he's been on an extended business trip. Then again, he'll be in the guest room, not in bed beside me."

"You could always invite him into the bed beside you," April said with a sly wink.

Scarlet responded with a nervous giggle. "Yeah, right. I'm sure he'd bite, because that won't complicate matters at all. Anyway, if my feminine wiles were that powerful, I wouldn't have lost him in the first place."

April ignored her sarcastic tone. "I still don't understand how you two could break up. You were the perfect couple. Your marriage was what I was striving for. Now you're divorcing and living in separate houses. It makes me feel very dubious about my own love life. I don't get it."

No relationship was perfect, although it might look like it from the outside. "We had issues. There were a few things that bothered me before the baby thing came up, but I thought we could work through it. In the end, I'm not the one who left, April. You'll have to ask Mason why he decided to give up. I know things between us had become…strained… And then he told me he wanted a divorce."

It had been only a couple months since their marriage unraveled, and the moment was still fresh and painful in her mind. She knew she hadn't been herself. Not since they lost Evan. But she'd been getting better. She was trying to reimagine her future without a child in it, and that took time to come to terms with.

"What reasons did he give for wanting the divorce?"

"He said he didn't want to hold me back from my dream of having a family. Since he was the one who couldn't have children, he said he thought it was best to step aside and let me find someone who could."

April's mouth fell open. "That's the most romantic breakup I've ever heard of."

Scarlet shook her head. "I don't know that I believe it was entirely selfless. It sounds noble, but I know Mason. He can't stand to fail at anything. Mason doesn't do well when he isn't on top. He'd rather walk away from something if he can't succeed. He's done it before. Did you know he was a vice president at his father's company before he quit and started the surf shop? That he dropped out of grad school? This was the same thing. Staying married to me would be a daily reminder that he failed and couldn't give me a child. And by that point, we'd started growing apart. If you'd asked me two years ago about us ever divorcing, I would've laughed in your face. But we'd become strangers living in the same house."

She knew most of that was her fault. Once they started to try having a family, she'd become obsessed with the idea. As the only child of two only children, Scarlet had always wanted a big family. Three or four kids at a minimum. For the first five years of their marriage, she and Mason had been focused on their careers and they'd been very successful. It wasn't until they decided to finally try for a family that things started to come apart.

Their passionate nights became dominated by ovulation kits and monthly disappointments. Then romance went out the window entirely in the face of sterile doctors' offices and medical exams that uncovered that Mason was infertile. It had been a huge blow to them both, but Mason seemed especially devastated by the diagnosis. She had tried to convince him that she didn't care, that they could adopt a child who needed a home. When that fell apart, too, they had no hope left for their marriage to cling to. At that point, Mason did what he always did—he made a decision without consulting her, and moved out.

"Do you think things will be different with him back in the house again? Now that he has custody of Luna, perhaps you could reconcile."

Scarlet didn't really think that was an option. Being back together would be awkward at best, contentious at worst. She imagined them tiptoeing around each other, trying to adapt to a new dynamic that flew in the face of nine years together. "This won't really be the right environment to rekindle our romance. We'll have Luna here. And the nanny."

April set down her empty wineglass and turned in her seat to look at Scarlet. "May I ask what the nanny is about?"

Scarlet's brow furrowed at her friend's silly question. "I'm on deadline. That massive humpback whale oil painting is due next week. You of all people should know that. And we're on the verge of opening up the Fisherman's Wharf gallery. That's going to keep me busy."

April didn't look convinced. "So busy that a woman desperate for children can't make time in her day to care for her orphaned niece, who needs a mother more than anything in the world?"

Scarlet frowned at her insightful friend. So she wasn't *that* busy. They would need help with Luna, though. She'd rather have an in-home nanny than put her in day care while they worked.

"Tell me that you're not putting up these walls as a self-preservation mechanism," April said.

"A what?" Scarlet snapped.

"You got attached to Evan and you lost him. Are you deliberately keeping distance between you and Luna so you don't get attached to her, too?"

That question hit a little closer to home than Scarlet cared for. Best friends saw too much sometimes. "It's not my baby, April, and Mason and I aren't reconciling. I know this whole thing seems like a terrible twist of fate that will reunite us and give us the child we've always wanted, but that's just not the case. Mason made it very clear to me that this is all for show, to put Jay at ease."

She sat back in her chair with a sigh. "Of course I love Luna as my niece, but no… I'm not going to let myself fall head over heels for her when Mason is her sole legal guardian. I basically have no rights in the matter. When he decides the time is right, he's going to take her away from me and carry on with his life. I'll be alone again, and brokenhearted, because he decided I need to go out and have a child of my own. No." She shook her head. "I'll do what he asked of me, but I can't let myself get attached to another child that isn't mine. That's why I refused to try adoption a second time after we lost Evan. I couldn't go through that again."

"So there's no chance whatsoever that you and Mason will call off the divorce and raise Luna together?" April looked at Scarlet with big, hopeful eyes.

Scarlet understood. It was a beautiful fantasy to have. They really had had a marriage that made other people jealous. They'd started out their careers together, had common goals and interests, and aesthetically they were a match made on a Hollywood film set. Losing Mason had been doubly hard because she really didn't think she'd ever find another relationship like that one. It was one of a kind and she hated to let it go, but she couldn't figure out how to hold on to it either.

She'd once held that kind of hope for her marriage, but she'd realized she was being naive. "No, April. While it might seem like our divorce was all about kids, it isn't that simple and adding a baby won't fix everything. Mason and I are not getting back together no matter how things might look."

Mason's gaze kept drifting from the white casket covered in pink roses to his wife and niece beside him. The service had been beautifully done. He was surprised, really, considering they had everything arranged for Jay and nothing arranged for Rachel. Fortunately, the funeral home had handled most of the details, and they'd purchased their plots months before after Jay's grim diagnosis.

To Mason's other side, Jay was seated in his wheelchair. It was hard for Mason to look at his younger brother. He was like a shriveled skeleton inside the black suit he'd worn last when he was fifty pounds heavier. A hospice nurse had come out with him to check on his oxygen and make sure he didn't overdo it. Even though it was July, he had a blanket over his lap and a pink rose clutched in his hand. All things considered, he was holding together pretty well.

Mason wished he could say the same about himself. On the outside he looked calm and collected enough, but on the inside he was a bundle of raw nerves. Just a glance at Jay or Scarlet was enough to set him on edge, and for very different reasons. He'd even done a shot of whiskey to get him through the service.

Every time he looked at his brother, he thought about Luna and the future he never expected. Being a father was an idea he'd taken for granted until it couldn't happen. Once he realized it wasn't in the cards for him, he'd let it go along with his marriage. The concept of being Luna's father once Jay was gone—and a single father at that—scared the hell out of him. Would he make the same choices Jay would've made for his daughter? Would he screw the kid up by levying the same unrealistic expectations of perfection on her the way his parents had done to him? That was the vicious cycle, right?

Each time he turned away from his brother, he caught a whiff of Scarlet's perfume on the air. He knew the scent well, having bought her a bottle of it every year on her birthday for the last nine years. The scent reminded him of her hair spilled across pillowcases, of his lips pressed against the hollow of her throat, tasting her pulse, and of her wrapped in nothing but a towel getting ready for the day.

He'd been desperate when he'd asked Scarlet to play house with him for a few weeks. Now a part of him regretted it. Leaving her the first time had been hard enough, but it was something he knew he had to do. Being back under the same roof might make it impossible to leave a second time. But he had no other choice. He couldn't give her what she needed, despite what she might say to the contrary.

Glancing over at her, he saw Scarlet weeping silent tears as she clutched baby Luna in her arms. They'd decided that their time as a reunited couple needed to start at the service so there was one less worry on Jay's mind. Once it was over, Mason would unload his stuff from the back of his Range Rover into the beach house. He'd also packed a bag at Jay's house with Luna's clothes and some toys. He'd move the rest of her belongings directly into his new place once the time came.

Thankfully, along with her stuff, Mason was also able to bring over Luna's nanny, Carroll. She was happy to stay with the baby and keep her job, which would ease the transition for everyone involved. It would also give Luna a familiar caregiver when her whole world was changing around her.

Who was going to help Mason as his whole world changed around him?

The pastor ended his short graveside sermon and began the commitment prayer. "We thank You for Rachel's life here on this earth, and we recognize that the body that lies before us is not Rachel, but rather the house in which she lived. We acknowledge that Rachel is rejoicing, even now, in Your very presence, enjoying the bless-ings of Heaven. Father, we commit her body to the earth, from which our bodies were originally created, and we rejoice in the fact that her spirit is even now with You. We thank You, Father, that in the days, weeks and months to come, these realities and the abiding presence of Your Spirit will especially strengthen, sustain and comfort Rachel's friends and family until they can join her there. In Jesus's name, amen."

The pastor gestured to Jay and the nurse rolled him forward to place his rose on top of her cas-ket. Jay placed his palm flat against the smooth white wood and closed his eyes. "I'll see you soon, baby."

Once he moved back, the pastor thanked every-one for coming and the crowd started to disperse so the team could complete the burial. With Jay needing to return immediately to the hospital, the family had opted against a wake, so it was done. Mason was relieved it was over, even though the next step he had to take might be even harder.

Mason squeezed Jay's shoulder. "We'll bring Luna to see you in a day or two, okay?"

His brother nodded and turned to the ambulance that had pulled into the cemetery. "My ride is here. Take good care of her."

Mason, Scarlet and Luna stood by the grave as the crowd cleared away and Jay was taken back to the hospital. When they could stall no longer, he turned back to her. "I guess we'd better go. I've got a lot of stuff to bring in and get settled."

Scarlet wiped her damp cheeks and nodded. Luna had fallen asleep in her arms. They walked to the car like the family everyone thought they were, loading Luna into her car seat and climbing into the front together.

Driving down the highway back to Malibu with Scarlet in the passenger seat and a baby in the back was a moment that brought back uncomfortable memories for Mason. It felt so easy, so normal, and yet it reminded him of Evan and their short stint as parents.

He'd thought they had a great marriage. He'd

had no doubt that they would be together forever. They complemented each other well, had common interests and were very compatible in their day-to-day lives. He enjoyed spoiling Scarlet. He could tell her anything without feeling judged. It was a far cry from the family he'd grown up in, where his father was always needling at him to push harder and do better. He'd meant well, of course, wanting Mason to succeed, but in the end, all he'd done was create a man with an inability to accept failure.

When they'd brought Evan home from the hospital, he had been only four days old. Mason remembered holding his son in his arms, looking at Scarlet and thinking their life was really complete now. Their perfect marriage had now become the perfect family, despite his inability to give her a child of their own. He'd started to think that perhaps he hadn't failed in this endeavor at all. Scarlet was happy, Evan had a loving family…things had worked out the way they were meant to.

It wasn't until they got the call from their attorney telling them that Evan's birth mother had changed her mind that he believed otherwise.

Scarlet pulled the gate opener out of her purse and Mason waited for it to open, allowing them to pull onto their property. "I'm going to put her down to finish her nap," she said, getting out of the car and unfastening Luna.

Mason went to the back of his SUV and opened the hatch. He hadn't packed much—a couple of suitcases' worth of clothes, toiletries and random items he might need, like his laptop and tablet.

As he stepped through the ground-floor entry of their former home, Mason hesitated. He'd moved on instinct up until this moment, but he realized things were different now. Some of the furniture had changed. His favorite chair and big-screen television had moved with him. There was a large floral arrangement on the dining room table in a vase that he didn't recognize and a bright-colored rug in the entry that was way too loud for his taste.

It was obvious this wasn't his house any longer and he wasn't sure where to go next. "Where am I sleeping?" he asked. Initially, he'd thought he'd be in the guest room, but that was where the nanny would sleep. Their four-bedroom house had a master suite, a nursery, a guest room and Scarlet's art studio.

Scarlet paused and turned to look at him. "I guess we'd better make that decision before the nanny arrives with her things. I think you'll have to sleep on the futon in my studio, with Carroll staying in the guest room that adjoins the nursery. Since my studio is upstairs near the master, it's probably a better choice anyway. Even the nanny will think that we're sharing a room."

"We can't just share a room?"

"Uh, no. I'm going along with this whole thing for Jay's sake, but if you think you're going to take liberties with me, you're wrong. I think it's best you sleep in the studio."

Although the idea of toughing it out on a futon didn't appeal to him, she was right. "I don't want to clutter your workspace. Will I be able to put my clothes and toiletries in your bathroom?"

"I suppose." Scarlet placed the sleeping baby into the Pack 'n Play they'd set up in the living room. "Just don't make a mess," she added with a smile.

Mason chuckled as he turned to the stairs and carried his bags up to the second floor. They both knew that Scarlet was the messy one. Mason was the oldest child, raised to the highest standards possible. He was as perfect as he could be. He was tidy. He cleaned up after himself. He always put his clothes in the hamper and his shoes on the rack. He even made the bed. Or at least his side if Scarlet was still in it.

Scarlet was an artist. She was an only child and was raised to be a free spirit. She saw nothing wrong with leaving a cereal bowl on the counter overnight or leaving a glob of toothpaste in the sink. Most of the time she was splattered in paint.

They were different, but he'd loved that about her. Really, Mason had been envious of her ability to let things go. In the few months they'd had Evan, Mason had been on edge over the mess. "Babies are messy," Scarlet would tell him with a happy smile even as she wiped away spit-up. He'd tried to loosen up then, but he had more than thirty years of training from his father to overcome.

At the top of the stairs, he turned toward the bedroom to unpack his clothes. He paused just inside the French doors, staring at the king-size bed he used to share with her. At least it looked like the same bed. She had changed the bedding to an ivory-and-purple floral print, and the walls had been painted a pale purple color that almost looked gray. It was a far more feminine room than he'd left behind.

It hadn't changed enough for him to forget everything that had happened in there, though. The sight of the headboard alone was enough to bring back the memories of passionate nights spent together in this very room. It made his whole body start to tighten in a way furniture shouldn't elicit.

Despite the ups and downs of their relationship, he and Scarlet had always enjoyed a very physical and satisfying love life. From the first time they'd made love on the beach at midnight to the final time the night before he decided to move out, they'd had that spark. Thoughts of that last night together flooded his mind and sent jolts of electricity south to other parts. That memory had haunted him the last few months, knowing he'd never touch her again that way and it was his own fault. His response tonight was compounded by the scent of her perfume, which was stronger in here than anywhere else in the house. It filled his lungs as he tried to take a deep breath and wish away his response to Scarlet.

"Carroll is here!" Scarlet called to him from downstairs.

"I'll be right down," he answered and set his bags to the side. He'd unpack later. Now he needed to focus on getting his body and mind on the same page or this would be a very uncomfortable few weeks.

Three

Scarlet couldn't shake the feeling that she was a horrible person.

It had been only three days since Mason, Luna and Carroll moved into her house, but she felt awful from virtually the moment it happened. Not because she didn't like having people in her space or that she resented the situation. It was because she did like it. She liked the scent of Mason's shampoo lingering in the heavy air of the bathroom after his shower. She liked hearing a baby's giggles downstairs. It reminded her of the happiest time of her life. And because of that, she had to keep her distance and close herself off from everyone else in the house.

And *that* was why she was a horrible person.

She hadn't held Luna since she laid her down for her nap after the funeral. She hadn't fed her, bathed her, played with her or even so much as stepped a foot into the nursery to check on her in the night. There might as well not even be a baby in the house. Scarlet tried to reason with herself that it was the nanny's job. That was why she'd insisted they have one, after all. Scarlet was just for show—a make-believe mom for a make-believe family, to soothe Jay's worries. So she could keep her distance, go along with her agreement with Mason and come out of this situation unscathed.

April was right—this plan was entirely centered on her self-preservation. But who could blame her? What woman with a ticking biological clock and a love of children wouldn't fall head over heels for Luna? She was the sweetest, most laid-back baby Scarlet had ever encountered. She had a head of crazy brown curls, Mason's big blue eyes and his dimples. There was plenty of Rachel and Jay in her, too, like Rachel's pert little nose and Jay's pouty mouth, but unfortunately all Scarlet could see were the bits of Mason's genetics in her.

The pieces that their own biological child would've had if they could have had their own.

It wasn't easy to keep her distance. It was just in her nature to want to care for people. When she heard a baby cry, she wanted to soothe it. When Mason swore, she wanted to rush down and see if he'd hurt himself. But she had to remind herself time and time again that this wasn't her baby and this wasn't her husband. If she let herself think otherwise, even for a moment, her heart would be crushed when it ended.

As it was, her heart still hadn't recovered from its last major hit. She wasn't entirely sure how she could recover when her too-sexy soon-to-be ex-husband was sitting on her couch watching a ball game and working on his laptop.

So far, she had made the excuse that she had to work. And it was true. In her studio, a massive three-panel canvas took up most of one wall, waiting to be painted. When she was done, it would be disassembled, photographed, boxed and shipped to Hawaii to hang in the lobby of the Mau Loa Maui hotel.

Scarlet took a step back and eyeballed her work. The painting was coming along. So far, she'd focused mainly on the background with the three humpback whales roughed in, but not yet done. Locking herself in her studio for hours on end had been helpful for that, at least. As long as she didn't glance over at the futon with Mason's neatly folded blankets and pajamas stacked on top of it.

She put down her paintbrush and stretched her hands out. Damn. It had been a long time since she'd worked such long stretches without stopping. How long had it been? Scarlet looked at her watch. It was almost seven in the evening. She hadn't even stopped to eat, drink or use the restroom since noon.

That was it for tonight. She rolled her shoulders and reluctantly stepped out into the hallway. She could hear the sounds of the television downstairs. It was about Luna's bedtime, so Carroll was probably giving her a bath.

Scarlet crept down the floating staircase and went into the kitchen. She was surprised to find Carroll there, making herself a cup of hot tea. Her face looked a little puffy and her nose was red. "Good evening, Mrs. Spencer," she said as though her nose were pinched closed.

Scarlet frowned. "You sound awful, Carroll. Are you coming down with something?"

Carroll shook her head. "I don't know. I hope not. I almost never get sick and I know now is a horrible time. You're so busy, and if I give this to Luna, she won't be able to visit her father at the hospital."

That was true. The chemotherapy had basically

destroyed Jay's immune system along with the cancer. Unfortunately, the cancer had recovered better than Jay had from the treatment. He would catch any bug he was exposed to and, at this point in his illness, a bout of the flu could be deadly for him.

Carroll set down her tea and launched into a fit of sneezes, followed by a rattling cough that Scarlet didn't like the sound of. She reached out to touch the woman's forehead and it was burning up.

"You've got a fever. I think you'd better take your tea and get to bed right now. I have some medicine upstairs you can take. I suggest you visit the walk-in clinic first thing in the morning. That flu medicine has to be administered within so many days of symptoms for it to work."

"What about Luna?"

That was a good question. What about Luna? Scarlet squeezed her eyes shut and resigned herself to her fate. She'd tried, she'd fought, but in the end, fate won out. "We can handle her until you're feeling better. I've made a lot of progress on my next painting."

Carroll's eyes grew wide. "No, no. Maybe I could call someone…"

Scarlet would have none of it. "No arguing. Now get to bed right this instant. Is Luna already down for the night?"

"No, ma'am. Mr. Spencer is playing with her on the deck. I asked him to keep her for a minute while I made tea."

That wasn't ideal. Scarlet was hoping the baby was already asleep so she could avoid the nursery for as long as possible, but she would do what she had to. "Okay. The two of us can take care of her until you feel better. Now, to bed!"

Scarlet watched as Carroll reluctantly carried her mug with her out of the kitchen toward her room. She steeled herself for what she had to do and went out to the deck to look for Mason and Luna, the two people she'd been trying to avoid.

The deck was empty, as was the pool. Curious, Scarlet walked around to the gate and steps that led to the beach. There, she found Mason and Luna playing in the sand. She stepped down to the beach, kicked off her shoes and walked through the sand to where they were playing.

The summer sun had finally set, but the sky was still bright and people still walked up and down the beach. There was a nice breeze for a summer's night, reminding Scarlet that she'd spent too much time working and not enough time enjoying the property they'd worked so hard to afford.

"Look, Luna. Your aunt Scarlet has come out to play with us!" Mason picked up the baby and turned her to face the house where Scarlet was walking toward them.

The baby immediately lit up when she saw Scarlet. She grinned wide and dropped her handfuls of sand to reach out for her.

"Someone has missed you," Mason said.

Scarlet stopped short, biting at her bottom lip. She ached to scoop the baby up into her arms and cradle her to her chest. To smell the top of her head and draw in the endearing scent that re-minded her of nights rocking Evan to sleep.

Instead, she crouched down out of arm's reach. Holding her during Rachel's funeral had been hard enough. "I doubt that," she said in a sooth-ing voice she used for babies. "What are we doing out here?"

"We are playing in the sand. I figured she's about to have a bath anyway, so why not?"

Scarlet nodded. "Well, it appears as though Nanny Carroll has the flu, so I've sent her to bed. This dirty little girl is ours to deal with for the next few days."

Luna reached down to pick up a little red plas-tic shovel and then dropped it. "Uh-oh!" she de-clared. So far, she'd mastered *mama, dada, no, uh-oh* and *dog.*

"Uh-oh is right," Mason repeated. "Are we going to be able to handle her on our own?"

"She's a baby, not a wild animal," Scarlet said. "I'm sure we'll be fine."

"And what about you?" he asked. His dark blue

eyes focused on hers, saying far more than his words ever would. "Will you be fine?"

Scarlet bit at her lip and stood up, dusting sand from her hands. "I guess we'll find out."

"Have you gone into the nursery yet?" Mason asked as he followed suit and lifted Luna into his arms.

For a moment, Scarlet was struck by the image in front of her. Her tall, strong Mason casually holding a baby in his arms. It was a simple thing—hardly unusual to any passersby—but it was enough to make her heart catch in her throat.

"No," she replied, turning away. As her gaze fell on the ocean, she spotted the splash of a pod of dolphins not far offshore. "Look!" She pointed out at the sea.

Mason turned and pointed the animals out to Luna. "Look, Luna. There are dolphins. They're jumping out of the water. Aren't they silly?"

Luna's eyes grew wide and her tiny little mouth formed an O of excitement. She started to clap enthusiastically as they watched them leap out of the water.

"They're dolphins. Can you say *dolphin*, Luna? *Doll-fin*."

"Dafin!" she exclaimed. "Dafin!"

Scarlet smiled, turning away from one of her favorite creatures on earth to look at Mason and Luna. The two of them together watching the sea with excited grins made her chest ache. This was the life she'd lost. The future she'd never have with him because he'd decided what was best for her instead of asking what she wanted.

"I think our job here is done," Mason said at last with a satisfied smirk. "She loves dolphins. Next, we just need to get her a baby wet suit and a surfboard."

Scarlet's smile dimmed a little. She remembered him making the same threats about teaching Evan to surf. The idea had terrified her at the time, although they'd never gotten that far. "I think she needs to master walking more than a few steps without falling down before she starts shooting the curl, don't you?"

Mason sighed with feigned disappointment. "I suppose. We need to get her in baby swimming lessons, though. She's already behind all the kids that started with those 'mommy and me' classes. She's going to be doing the backstroke before her second birthday."

Scarlet just shook her head and headed back to the house with Mason and Luna on her heels. "Don't tell Jay about all this. He'll think you're out to drown his baby."

"Don't be silly, Scarlet. If Luna knows the backstroke, there's no way she'll drown."

Mason awoke with a start. It took a moment for him to get his bearings in the dark, unfamiliar room. Then, from the crick in his back, he remembered that he was on the futon in Scarlet's studio.

Then the wail of a baby sounded louder and he realized what had woken him up. He was about to fling back the sheets and go downstairs, but he heard footsteps down the hallway and Scarlet's soothing voice. "I'm coming, Lulu. I'm coming, baby girl."

Mason held his breath, waiting to see what would happen. The night before, Scarlet had let him give Luna a bath and put her to bed. In exchange, she'd made some dinner for them both while he was doing it. If he was right, she was about to step into the nursery for the first time in a year.

He got up and crept across the floor as quietly as he could, then peered out the door. Luna's bedroom was near the foot of the stairs. He saw Scarlet stand there for a moment, just outside the threshold. Then she took a deep breath and stepped inside. After a few seconds, the crying stopped and he could make out the calming mumbles Scarlet said to soothe her.

A few minutes later, Scarlet came out of the bedroom with Luna in her arms. He watched them go into the living room, where Scarlet sat in her favorite chair to rock Luna back to sleep. He remembered her doing the same with Evan. It had worked like a charm every time.

After about ten minutes, he moved quietly down the stairs. "Is everything okay?" he asked in a hoarse whisper.

Scarlet nodded and continued to rock. Luna was snuggled in her arms, already sleeping. "We just needed a new diaper and someone to love on us a little bit."

Mason settled onto the couch beside her. He watched the way Scarlet looked down at the sleeping baby and immediately understood why she'd chosen to be so closed off the last few days. It was to keep from falling in love with the sweet bundle in her arms. She looked at Luna the same way she'd looked at Evan, as though the sun rose and set on that tiny baby.

He'd thought at first that she just didn't want to be around her. Scarlet had made it very clear after they lost Evan that she didn't want to try adoption again. She couldn't risk falling for another baby only to lose it. He understood that. He didn't really think of Luna that way, but he supposed in Scarlet's eyes it was the same. It wasn't her child, so she wasn't going to get attached. Scarlet wanted her very own baby; he knew that. Perhaps spending this time with Luna would light the fires in her to settle down with someone else and start a family.

"Motherhood always did look good on you," he said without thinking.

Scarlet froze for a moment, staring at him before taking a breath and gazing back down at the sleeping baby. "Christian Dior always looks good on me, too, but that doesn't mean I should wear it all the time."

"What is that supposed to mean?" he asked, speaking louder than he expected to.

Scarlet raised a finger to her lips, then gingerly stood up. "I'm going to put her back to bed before I answer that question."

Mason waited as she returned Luna to her crib and shut the nursery door. When she came back, she beckoned for him to follow her out onto the deck. He stood up and traced her steps, noticing for the first time that she was wearing nothing more than a tiny pink cotton chemise with lacy white trim. It fit tightly to her full bust, then flowed freely over her hips to midthigh. It wasn't exactly lingerie, but it wasn't your grandmother's nightgown either.

He found himself instantly responding to the innocent outfit as though it were some racy black teddy. His pulse started racing and his mouth was suddenly bone-dry. He attempted to lick his lips, but it didn't help. It only made him think about her lips and how long it had been since he'd kissed them. Too long.

After he stepped outside, Scarlet pulled the glass door closed behind them. The sky was an inky black sprinkled with as many stars as the LA lights would allow. The moon was hovering overhead, almost full, casting a silvery glow to Scarlet's figure.

"What I meant was that just because something

looks good on you doesn't mean you get to wear it. Motherhood might suit me, but it appears that life may have other plans."

Mason frowned. "I don't know why you would say that. You've got plenty of time to still be a mother, Scarlet. You're beautiful and talented… Surely you'll meet a man who will give you the family that you want."

Scarlet looked at him as though he'd reached out and slapped her. "Stop saying that."

"Stop saying what? It's true. That's why…" He trailed off. *That's why I left you.*

Scarlet crossed her arms over her chest, pressing her breasts up against the deep V of her nightgown. "I don't know why you think that just because you're divorcing me I'm going to waltz out the door and find another man I'll love as much as I loved you. Do you think they just have men lined up at the shopping mall and I pick one out and live happily ever after?"

Mason tried not to note her use of the past tense where he was concerned. He was the one who left, but that didn't mean he had to like the idea of her moving on. "Don't be silly," he said. "I'm trying to be serious here. I don't want you to give up on your dream of having your own family, Scarlet. Not because of me. You can still have it. Sure, it won't drop in your lap tomorrow, but you can have it."

"Maybe. Someday. But I sure as hell can't move on with you here. It's so hard to have you here and not think about everything else. About us. About Evan. About what a mess our lives have become…"

"Do you think it's any easier on me? Christ, Scarlet. The last three days have been torture."

Scarlet flinched. "This is what you wanted. How has it been torture?"

He ran his fingers through his sleep-tousled hair and then rubbed his palm over his face. "Do you know how hard it is for me to be around you and not want you? I am crazy with wanting you. You're my wife."

"I *was* your wife," she said in a cold, accusatory tone she'd never used during their marriage. "You *left* me."

"I left you because I can't have you, Scarlet. Not and let you have what you need to be happy."

She narrowed her gaze at him and took a step closer. "How do you know what I need, Mason? You always do this. You've always treated me like I'm a part of the company that you have to manage. You're always making decisions for me, thinking you know what's best, instead of asking me what I want or listening to me when I tell you things."

Mason hesitated in his reply. He knew it probably seemed that way. He did listen. He just didn't believe her. No matter how many times she said she was okay not having children, he knew it was a lie. She was settling. Because of him. And he wasn't about to let her do that for something so important. Even when he didn't like what he had to do, he'd do it because it was in her best interests.

"You bought this house without asking me."

"I bought your dream house on Malibu. You don't like it?"

"I love it," she argued. "But what if I didn't? You never consult me. You chose our honeymoon. You hired Nanny Carroll without asking me what I thought. You bought me that Mercedes and just left it in the driveway."

"You don't like your Mercedes?"

Scarlet sighed. "That's not the point. The point is that you never consult me on anything. You just make a decision. It's not just about the car. Or the divorce. It's everything. You never ask what I want."

He took a step closer to her, leaving only a few inches between them. When he was this near to her, he could feel the warmth of her skin and her soft breath on his lips. "So what do you want, Scarlet?"

She placed her hand against his chest and looked up at him with her large dark eyes that spoke volumes even as she stood silent. He prayed she couldn't feel his heart pounding in his rib cage or hear the blood rushing through his veins at top speed. That, combined with the nearby crashing of the waves, was a dull roar that filled his ears. Mason kept his hands at his sides. They curled into fists as he fought to hold still and keep from sweeping her into his arms.

That was the absolute wrong thing to do. Right? He'd distanced himself from her intentionally. Filed for divorce. Moved out of the house. All to give them both a chance to start over. Except he didn't want to start over. Not really. But being around Scarlet stirred up so many confusing emotions inside of him. Among the desire, he also fought the feelings of inadequacy and frustration that he couldn't shake. As much as he wanted to be around Scarlet, he also wanted to stay away from her. That wasn't what a marriage was supposed to be like. He was convinced they would be happier apart than together.

And yet, if she leaned in and kissed him right now, he wouldn't stop her.

"What if I said I wanted you to kiss me?" she asked.

Mason squeezed his eyelids tightly shut to block out the image of her looking up at him with those full lips and sad eyes. It was as though she could sense his weakness and knew that she was it. Why else would she ask for the one thing he was reluctant to give her? The one thing he was desperate to give her?

The hand on his chest lifted, but before Mason could open his eyes, he felt her palm against his cheek. She softly caressed his face, letting her thumb drag across his bottom lip. "Aren't you going to say anything?" she asked.

"It's not what I want to say, Scarlet, it's what I want to do."

She moved closer to him, pressing her firm breasts against his chest. Her whole body was perfectly aligned with his, reminding him of how she was the perfect fit for him in so many ways. This close, he had no doubt that she could feel his desire for her through the thin cotton of his lounging pants.

"What do you want to do, Mason?"

He couldn't hold back any longer. His eyes flew open to look down at her before the floodgates gave way. "This," he said.

Lunging forward, he scooped her face into his hands and pulled her mouth to his. They collided with the passionate force of a nuclear blast. Weeks and months of frustration, tears and need coursed through his veins as he threatened to devour her. Her mouth was open to him and her lips were soft, just as they always were. His hands were nearly shaking with the rush of adrenaline that came from finally being able to touch her again. The taste of her, the scent of her skin, the soft whimper against his lips…it was everything that he'd thought about, fantasized about, in all the weeks he'd lain alone in his new house in the Hollywood Hills. Scarlet was addictive and quitting her cold turkey had left him miserable and wanting.

But wouldn't this just make it worse?

Fighting his instincts, Mason pulled away, leaving Scarlet unsteady and gasping for breath. What was he doing? They'd gone through so much to put an end to this and here he was, practically attacking her on the back deck. This was why he'd kept his distance from her. Why he needed to continue keeping his distance from her. He had no self-control where Scarlet was concerned.

"What's the matter?" she asked.

Mason could only shake his head. "Things are so complicated for us, Scarlet. I just don't think what we're doing is going to help matters."

"And lying to everyone while we pretend to be a happy family will help?" With a sad shake of her head, Scarlet turned back to the house and disappeared through the sliding glass door.

With a curse, Mason dropped down into one of the deck chairs. He cradled his head in his hands and prayed that his body could forget just how badly it wanted her.

Four

Despite her late night with Mason, Scarlet found herself awake just as the sun came up. She sat for a moment, reliving the thrill of his kiss and the sting of his words, before she realized she needed to get up and try to put last night behind her. Despite their attraction to one another, which had never waned, he was right about their relationship being so complicated.

Over time, it had simply become one of those situations where being together hurt more than being apart. Seeing each other was just a reminder of everything that had gone wrong. At least for Mason. He intended to maintain his distance while they were stuck in this situation together, and so she needed to respect that, no matter how fast he made her heart race and her skin tingle from his touch. Attraction didn't solve any of their issues.

She wrapped up in her silk robe and crept downstairs as quietly as she could. As she did every morning, she started a pot of coffee, took her vitamins and stared blankly into the refrigerator for something to eat. When she found nothing, she shut the fridge and found herself looking at the nursery door just beyond it.

Last night, with Luna crying, she'd ignored the sense of anxiety that normally kept her from going inside that room. She'd suppressed it all, scooped the crying infant from her crib, changed her diaper and run out into the living room as quickly as she could. She hadn't allowed herself to look around at the cheery blue walls, the stuffed animals on the shelves or the fabric sign over the crib that read "Evan." She didn't need to. She knew every inch of that room despite having not gone in it in nearly fourteen months.

This morning, there was no baby crying. No reason for her to charge in. Even so, she wanted to check on Luna while the coffee was brewing. She went to the door and stopped. It was harder than she'd expected to reach out and grab the doorknob without Luna's cry urging her on. It was a simple action, yet an important one for her. The only sound in the whole house seemed to be her heart pounding in her chest as she moved her hand closer. As her fingers wrapped around the cold metal, she hesitated again.

Scarlet didn't know why this room meant so much. Why it was so important. It felt like all she had left of Evan, but that wasn't really true. He wasn't in that room. It was just wasted space filled with unused baby things. At least that was what Mason had tried to tell her.

A few months after they lost Evan, he'd encouraged her to redecorate. If they weren't going to try to adopt again, what was the point of keeping it a nursery? They could turn it into a home gym. Or a library. Or a storage room. He didn't care, as long as it wasn't a pale blue shrine to the child they'd lost. Scarlet had been aghast at the mere suggestion. That was where the conversation had stopped until Luna needed a place to stay.

He was right. She knew that. Taking a deep breath, Scarlet turned the knob, allowing the door to click open. The early-morning sunlight streamed in through the window, highlighting the crib and the very awake baby in it. Luna had used the rails of her crib to pull herself up and was standing there with a slobbery grin on her face when she saw Scarlet. Apparently, the baby was a morning person.

"What are you doing awake?" Scarlet asked.

Luna immediately started babbling and bouncing up and down while she held to the rail. Scarlet couldn't suppress her grin as she watched her niece. She had always been such a happy baby. It was unthinkable that she should have so much tragedy in her life so early. She supposed it was good that Luna wouldn't remember any of it, but at the same time, she also wouldn't remember what a good mother Rachel was, or how much Jay doted on his baby girl.

That was the thought that propelled Scarlet one step, then two steps into the nursery.

As she got closer, Luna reached out to her to be picked up. Without her grip on the crib, she lost her balance and fell backward, hitting her head with a loud crack on the wooden crib back. The grin vanished, followed by a loud howl of pain and fear. Scarlet didn't hesitate to rush forward and scoop Luna into her arms. The baby was instantly red-faced with tears streaming down her fat cheeks.

"Mama-a-a!" Luna wailed, making Scarlet's chest ache as she thought about the mama who wouldn't come.

Scarlet cradled Luna against her breast, rubbing her back and mumbling the first soothing words that came to mind as they rocked back and forth. Gently, she let her hand smooth over the back of Luna's head as she checked for a cut or a scrape, but she didn't find any. Luna might have a bit of a knot in a few hours, but mostly she'd just scared herself taking a tumble.

After just a few minutes with Luna curled up in her arms, the sobbing finally subsided. When Scarlet looked down, Luna was watching her with big blue eyes that were so much like Mason's. Both he and Jay had the same unusually blue eyes and Luna had inherited them from her daddy. She also had the dark curly hair and dimples of the Spencer side of the family. Scarlet imagined that a stranger would have no problem thinking Mason was Luna's father.

It made her chest tighten to think that any babies they could've had would have looked like Luna. They would've made beautiful babies if they'd been granted the ability to do so. As she looked down at her, Luna reached her fingers up to touch Scarlet's face. Her eyes started to tear up at the innocent gesture and she felt the last of her resolve starting to crumble.

It wasn't supposed to be like this. She was supposed to keep her distance so she didn't get too attached to another baby she couldn't keep. This baby was going to be raised by her husband. Her future ex-husband. Not her. That meant she was at a high risk of getting her heart broken again, the one thing she swore she'd never let herself do. Scarlet knew how she was—any baby turned her to butter. A beautiful, happy baby who needed a mother more than anything in the world? That was impossible to resist. Perhaps she was wasting energy fighting it.

Once Luna was soothed, Scarlet was able to take a deep breath and realize that she'd been standing in the nursery for a good five minutes. Nothing had happened. It was just a room filled with furniture and things. The specter of her lost baby didn't haunt her the way she thought it would. It was a relief, and yet the relief was tempered by the fear that she was happily embarking on another path to heartache.

Looking down at Luna, Scarlet realized there was nothing she could do about it. She could try to stay objective, try to remember that this situation was temporary, but telling herself that she could resist this baby girl was a damn lie. She wanted to smell her baby shampoo and rock her until she fell back to sleep.

In fact, she decided to do just that. Scarlet walked over to the rocking recliner and sat down for the first time since she'd handed over her adopted son to child services.

Sitting in the rocker with him had been one of her favorite things. Some nights, Mason had to force her to put Evan in his crib because she wanted to just stay in her chair and hold him all night while he slept. Cradling Luna in her lap now felt different, but still good.

Before long, Luna had drifted back to sleep and Scarlet felt her own eyelids getting heavy.

She closed her eyes for what seemed like a second and a half.

"Scarlet?" a voice whispered.

She opened her eyes and saw Mason standing in the doorway of the nursery. He looked just as surprised to see her in the nursery as she was to see him fully dressed in one of his suits and surrounded by late-morning sunlight. Scarlet winced at the glare coming through the window where there had only been soft dawn light a moment before. "What time is it?"

"After eight. I've got to go into the office today. Carroll just left to see the doctor. Will you be okay with Luna by yourself? Do I need to call someone to help?"

She hadn't just blinked; she and Luna had both dozed hard for almost two hours. She'd slept better in this chair holding her than she had in months. In a year, even. How was it that having a baby in her arms made her so much more contented and relaxed? Suddenly, it felt silly for her to demand a nanny around to care for Luna while they were staying with her. She obviously didn't need the help. It was only to keep her from getting too close. She feared that was an unavoidable risk, nanny or no.

"No, we don't need help. I'm sure we'll be okay," Scarlet said.

Mason watched her curiously for a moment, narrowing his gaze at the two of them sitting in her rocking chair. "You're sure? I could call Mom."

Scarlet shook her head vigorously. "Don't you dare drag your mother into this. Really, just go. We'll be fine. I think we'll have some Cheerios and maybe a little fruit, then go play on the beach for a bit. It looks like a clear, sunny day for splashing in the ocean. Maybe we'll even get in the pool if it's warm enough."

"Okay." Mason seemed reluctant, but whatever was going on at work would trump his concerns. It always did. You didn't turn a single store into a national chain by sitting idly by and letting things evolve naturally. "I'll see you later this afternoon. Call me if you need anything," he said before slipping from the doorway and disappearing down the hall.

With him gone, Scarlet looked at Luna. She was awake now and chewing on one slobbery fist. With all that chewing and drooling, she was probably getting some more teeth. She made a mental note to check Luna's bag for a teething ring she could put in the freezer. "I think someone is hungry. What do you say we get that diaper changed, find us both an outfit for today and have some breakfast? Does that sound good to you?"

"Dafin!" Luna said.

"Dolphin?" Scarlet repeated. She was surprised Luna remembered her new word from yesterday. Seeing them must have made quite an impression on her. "Do you want to go see the dolphins again?"

Luna just grinned, showing off the four little baby teeth that had come in up front. That looked like a yes to her. Scarlet stood up and laid Luna out on the changing table. She unsnapped her onesie pajamas and put on a clean diaper. As she pulled on the last of the new outfit she'd chosen for her, Scarlet eyed the nursery wall. The wall the crib was on had no windows. It was just a big expanse of blue with Evan's name sign strung across it.

It was time for that to come down, Scarlet decided. She propped Luna on her hip and reached up to unhook the ribbon that was tied around one nail, then the other. The plush fabric letters fell to the floor in a heap. She held her breath as she looked back up at the now bare wall for the first time since they'd hung that sign over a year ago.

It felt good. She thought she might burst into tears at the sight of Evan's sign crumpled on the ground, but it actually made her feel as though a weight had been lifted from her chest. Mason had been right, although she wouldn't ever admit that to him.

Taking a step back, she looked around the room. There were some other things in here that were due for a change—baby boy clothes that could be donated, some toys that Luna was too old to be interested in, all that could go to make room for more of Luna's things. And as for the big empty wall, Scarlet had an idea brewing for that.

With a satisfied smirk, Scarlet looked at Luna. "I think we're going to do a little redecorating today."

Luna grinned and clapped her chubby little hands together. She was a girl after Scarlet's own heart.

It ended up being a longer day at the office than Mason anticipated. He had planned to help take care of Luna so Scarlet wouldn't feel over-whelmed with Carroll gone, but he couldn't get away, and then he got stuck in the infamous LA traffic.

Mason wasn't quite sure what he was going to come home to that day, but he never would've bet on what he actually found. Carroll's car was still gone, making Mason nervous that Scarlet had been alone with Luna all day. He rushed through the front door, then stopped to listen. The living room and kitchen were empty and quiet. He couldn't see anyone through the wall-to-wall windows along the back of the house, so they weren't outside on the deck. Then he heard a giggle.

He set down his briefcase by the door and slipped out of his suit coat. He tossed it over the back of a chair as he made his way toward the nursery. There, he stopped short.

Finding Scarlet in the nursery that morning had been a surprise. Finding Scarlet back in the nursery—this time on a stepladder with a paint-brush in her hand—was another matter entirely. She was wearing a tank top and a pair of cutoff shorts that made her legs look four feet long. Her hair was pulled up into a messy knot on top of her head, exposing the long line of her neck and shoulders. She wasn't wearing makeup or even a bra as she worked, but Mason was captivated by her as usual.

Seeing her like this reminded him of the early days in their marriage when he would interrupt her work because he couldn't stand not to make love to her right that second. Things had been so easy between them then. Children were a far-off idea, not a recent source of constant heartache. It made him want to go back to the times when he could use his fingertip to play connect the dots with the tiny splatters of blue and green paint that decorated her pale skin after she worked.

Luna squealed, drawing his attention to where she was sitting and dousing any thoughts of messing around with his estranged wife. Luna was buckled into a bouncy chair on the floor, playing with a Taggies blanket that she seemed to prefer over her head. Behind her was all the nursery furniture that Scarlet had moved to the opposite wall so she had room to paint the mural.

Not just any mural, but a Scarlet Spencer original of dolphins swimming in an enchanting underwater scene. There was kelp drifting through the water like undersea trees, colorful schools of fish and coral providing highlights against the dark blues and greens of the water...and two half-painted dolphins as the centerpiece of the scene.

Scarlet had done a couple large-scale murals on the sides of aquariums and such, but she'd turned down repeated requests to paint a mural in a private residence. It made sense that the first one she did was in her own home, though. He just wondered why it had taken over seven years for her to think about doing it here.

Mason had always loved watching her work. When she was painting, her focus was 100 percent on her piece. Her canvases were typically so large that painting was almost like a ballet for her—reaching and turning and flicking her wrists to apply color in just the right place. When they had Evan, she switched to nontoxic paints and put an air purifier in her studio because she couldn't stand being apart from him long enough to work. She would swaddle him in a Boba Wrap, tucked against her chest, and he would sleep happily while she painted. Watching them move together was one of the most beautiful things he'd ever seen.

And watching her try to paint after they lost him was one of the most heartbreaking things he'd ever witnessed. He was suffering from the loss of their son, too, but somehow watching Scarlet go through her stages of grief had been harder than feeling it himself. Perhaps because he blamed himself for all of it. Somehow, he'd managed to hurt—not even hurt, nearly destroy—the one person he loved more than anything else. More than himself. That was why he'd walked away to give her a chance to be happy.

Capturing this perfect moment made him glad to see her so light of spirit again, but it also scared him. Was bringing Luna into her life temporarily going to hurt her again? Was coming back here with Luna going to ruin everything he'd done to help Scarlet move on with her life?

He hadn't thought about it that way when he asked her to play along with the marriage for Jay's sake. He'd only been focused on his grieving brother. When Scarlet took a distant stance from him and Luna, he'd almost been offended by it. But now that he saw what it truly meant for her to let her guard down and let Luna, at least, into her life, he understood how much he'd really asked of her.

He felt guilty, but it was too late to change it now. All he could do was hope that being with Luna for a few weeks would help her heal and move on from losing Evan. Maybe it would even inspire her to find that new family with someone who could give her the biological children that she wanted.

Mason watched Scarlet dip her brush into a gray paint and start to fill in the space where one of the dolphins would be. He knew from watching her that there would be layer after layer of color and highlight on top of this, but it was a start. Considering she'd begun the mural when he left for work, she was moving along amazingly fast. That typically took a big dose of inspiration for Scarlet.

"Wow," he said, the words slipping from his lips.

Scarlet's brush hand stiffened and pulled away before she turned to look at him. She smiled and set the brush on the tray so it didn't drip down the wall and ruin her work. "Hello there. I didn't hear you come in. Luna and I have been very busy today."

"I noticed. What's all this about?" he asked.

Scarlet climbed slowly down the stepladder and wiped her hands on the jean shorts that were already speckled with a million different colors of paint. Before she could answer, Luna pointed at the wall and said, "Dafin!"

They both looked at Luna and smiled wide. "That, right there," Scarlet said, "is what it's all about. That's all she's been saying since she saw that pod yesterday. Today I decided that this room needs a face-lift and who better to paint her a mural with dolphins than me?"

It all seemed perfectly logical when she said it, and if he hadn't battled with Scarlet for months over changing this very same room, he might be able to follow along. Instead, his gaze fell on the stack of boxes and bags in the corner. Evan's things. "What about all that?" He gestured to the pile.

Scarlet followed his gaze and nodded. "We're starting fresh. Luna isn't going to use any of that stuff, so I decided to donate it to someone who could. Right now, it's just in her way. Isn't it?"

She turned her attention to Luna in her bouncy chair. Luna grinned and flung her Taggies blanket out of reach. Scarlet unsnapped Luna's safety belt and lifted her up out of the seat. As she held her, Luna reached out to touch a smear of dried blue paint across Scarlet's cheek.

"Am I messy?" she asked, but the baby just grinned. Instead, she turned to Mason. "Do I need to hose down in the yard?"

"It's not that bad. I think the shower will be adequate."

Scarlet frowned and walked over to the mirror that was attached to the dresser. "You're a liar. I'm an absolute mess."

Mason just shrugged. "You know I always liked you messy. Just like you always liked me with saltwater hair and wet-suit tan lines."

Scarlet smiled for a moment, both of them thinking back to the happier times where painting, surfing and being in love had been the center of their lives and their marriage. Then her smile slowly faded and she rubbed absently at her cheek. "I'd better get in the shower," she said.

"I'll take Luna," he offered. "Where's Carroll?"

Scarlet handed the baby over to him and he noticed just how careful she was not to touch him in the process. He supposed that was his own fault after the way he reacted the night before. It wasn't that he didn't want to touch her. He wanted that more than anything. Kissing her last night had relit a fire inside him that he'd tried unsuccessfully to squash the last few months. If he didn't walk away then, he knew that he would want to touch her, make love to her…and then where would they be? He wanted Scarlet; he just knew that he shouldn't want her. Even then, he couldn't help but feel slighted by her avoidance.

"She has the flu. She got the medicine, but the doctor said she's contagious for another twenty-four hours, so she's staying with her sister. She's hoping she'll be back tomorrow afternoon. The day after at the latest."

Whether it was good or bad for Scarlet's situation, he had to admit he was relieved that she was okay caring for Luna. Mason wasn't entirely sure what he would do in this scenario if the nanny was sick and he had to take care of the baby on his own. He had been thrown into the deep end of the parenting pool without warning or a life preserver. Scarlet was all he had to cling to in a time like this and he was very grateful for her help.

"It sounds like you deserve a treat. How about after your shower, we go to Rico's for dinner? That's still your favorite, right? We can relax, have some good food, a nice night out just the three of us."

Scarlet looked at him curiously before nodding slowly. "It's still my favorite. Are you sure you want to do that, though? We could just as easily order takeout. We'll have to play the public couple if we go out and run into someone we know."

That was true. They really hadn't had to try since the funeral. Carroll didn't seem too interested in their business at home. "To be honest, we've been apart for such a short time compared to how long we were together, it's easier to pretend to be a couple than to try to be apart. Unless you mind...?" He stopped, waiting for her to say she didn't want to be seen in public with him.

"No, I don't mind."

With a sigh of relief, he smiled. "Then go get ready."

"Okay." Scarlet smiled and disappeared up the stairs to the master suite.

Mason watched her climb the staircase, her cut-off shorts creeping higher with every step. His mind easily made the leap to running his hands over her smooth skin and wrapping those legs around his waist. He'd missed that. Missed her.

Then Mason looked at Luna and cursed silently. He didn't know what he was thinking, fantasizing about Scarlet like that. Just because she had warmed up to Luna didn't mean that they were on their way to being one big, happy family. Scarlet still wanted and needed her own family. They were just pretending, and when Jay was gone, they'd both go back to living their own separate lives.

The wheels of their divorce continued to turn, no matter how attracted they might be to each other or how natural it felt to be in the same house again. They were miles away from raising Luna together.

And it was his own fault.

Five

"Do you want dessert?"

Scarlet looked at him and shook her head. "Not only am I full enough to burst, but this one is about to pass out in her high chair."

They both glanced over at Luna. Her eyes were getting heavy and she was weaving steadily in her seat. It was a late night for her. Dinner had been nice, but it hadn't been a fast process. He hadn't really considered that when he chose this place. They'd never attempted to come here as a family before with Evan, so time hadn't really been a factor he'd considered. Thankfully, Luna hadn't fussed once. She was happy in her chair with a bottle, some finger nibbles and her favorite stuffed bunny.

"I bet she's going to be asleep before we leave the parking lot," he said. "If she lasts that long."

Mason paid the tab and, when they were ready, lifted Luna up out of her high chair. She curled against his chest, resting her head on his shoulder. On instinct, he pressed a kiss to her forehead. She had that baby smell he remembered from giving Evan baths—a distinct mix of milk and baby shampoo.

It reminded him that he hadn't really spent that much time caring for Luna. Carroll was doing most of the work, with Scarlet filling in for her while she was sick. Thank goodness Scarlet had stepped up. A nanny was nice, but they couldn't be there every second, as this bout of flu had proven. Scarlet had been the one to take on most of Evan's care while he worked long hours expanding his business into Florida. He didn't know a thing about babies, really. He didn't know what he would've done without her.

Hopefully, Carroll would continue on with him once they moved to his place in the Hills, but he would need to work on a secondary backup option, as well. Scarlet wouldn't always be there to bail him out. He might be doing okay with a happy, sleepy baby, but a cranky one, a fussy one, or basically any other ailment that caused a baby to scream or spew fluids…he'd be thoroughly clueless.

He stopped just as they reached the front door and found Scarlet watching him with a curious look on her face. "What?" he asked. "Is she drooling on my lapel?"

"No, your suit coat is fine. You two just look sweet together. She's so comfortable there that she's already fallen asleep in your arms," Scarlet said as she propped open the door and they stepped outside the restaurant.

"I always had a way with the ladies."

"You put them to sleep?" Scarlet asked with a grin.

"Pretty much. You stayed awake, though, so I married you."

Scarlet opened the car door so Mason could fasten Luna into her car seat. "So, that was the determining factor, eh? I thought it was my sparkling personality."

Mason shut the door and turned to look at her. Scarlet was leaning against the driver's-side door with her arms crossed, surveying him. Her wavy hair was loose around her shoulders, covering the bare skin that her flimsy strappy top exposed. For some reason, she looked younger tonight. More like the girl he'd fallen in love with at the beach. That Scarlet never looked at him with disappointment in her eyes the way his wife Scarlet did.

It took everything he had not to reach out and touch her. He wanted to brush a strand of dark hair from her eyes, run his fingertips down her bare arm and kiss her against the side of his Range Rover until she was breathless. His brain just couldn't seem to convince his body that she wasn't his any longer.

"Your sparkling personality certainly helped." He leaned into her, bracing his hand on the roof of the car. "So did the fact that you were beautiful, talented, smart and yet stupid enough to be attracted to me. I had to jump on that before some other guy snatched you up."

Scarlet smiled, then reached out to touch his face. It was a simple, casual touch, and yet it made his blood heat in his veins until he was forced to loosen his tie.

"I've missed you, Mason."

Mason couldn't think of a smarter response in the moment while she was touching him, so he opted for honesty. "I've missed you, too." He had. More than he ever expected to. Every night he had to convince himself not to call her. She couldn't move on if he didn't get out of her life.

"What happened to us?" she asked. "I would've told anyone who would listen that you and I would be together for the long haul. And here we are, on the verge of finalizing our divorce. Sometimes I look around our empty house and wonder what the hell went wrong."

"I let you down," Mason said. "That's what happened."

Scarlet's dark eyes widened and caught the reflection of the parking lot lights. She seemed surprised by his words, although he didn't know why. It seemed obvious to him.

"You let me down? Are you serious?"

Mason flinched at her words. "Yes, I'm serious. You and I both know that our problems started when I couldn't give you the children you wanted."

Scarlet's hand moved from his face to his chest, where it pressed insistently. "You stop right there. We've already had this fight ten times, but you don't ever seem to listen to me when I tell you that I don't blame you for that. Yes, I wanted children, but you certainly didn't let me down. It's out of your control. Life doesn't always work out the way you expect it to, Mason. You've got to roll with the punches."

"And our attempt at adoption was certainly a one-two punch to the gut."

Scarlet sighed and shook her head. "We had some bad luck, that's true. I'll admit that it scared me enough not to want to try adoption a second time. But again, that isn't your fault. You know that, right? There's nothing we could've done to convince the judge once Evan's birth mother changed her mind. I feel like I've been talking to a wall for the last year and nothing I say or do has any impact on you aside from just pushing you further away."

She might not blame him, but he certainly blamed himself. "You aren't pushing me away. I left all on my own."

Scarlet's hand dropped to her side, stealing the warmth of her body from his chest. "I know. You've made that clear, but it doesn't make any sense to me. Tell me the real reason why you left me because I still don't understand."

Mason looked Scarlet in the eye, but the pained expression on her face stole the words from his lips. She looked tired, older in that moment, like the last few years weighed as heavily on her shoulders as they did on his own. He hated that he was the one responsible for it.

She did deserve an answer, though. They'd never really had this fight. Not exactly. After everything happened with Evan, they'd just drifted apart until they were two people moving around one another in the same house. Their conversations never seemed to stray beyond what they would have for dinner and when the trash needed to be taken to the curb. That wasn't a marriage and he knew it. He just didn't know what to do about it.

"I told you before. I left...to give you a chance at happiness."

"Bullshit."

Scarlet's sharp words startled Mason from his next response. "What?" he asked instead.

Her face flushed as red as her name as she

shook her head. "Don't you dare walk away from our marriage and then have the audacity to tell me that you did it for me. This is not what I wanted. This is not what I asked for. Yes, I wanted a family, but until you walked out that door, Mason, *you* were my family. Now I have nothing. No baby, no husband."

"But you have the hope of something better than what I could give you. A month, a year, even two years from now, the right man could walk into your life and give you everything you wanted."

"And what if all I really wanted was to be happy?" she asked. "With you."

Mason was at a loss for words. He had a hard time believing she really, truly felt that way. She might now, but in fifteen years when her opportunity had passed, she would resent him. He didn't want his wife to harbor animosity toward him, now or in the future.

"If I thought I could make you happy, I'd tear those divorce papers up in a heartbeat."

Scarlet stood silent and still as she watched his face. He couldn't tell whether she was hoping he would call off the divorce or was terrified by the idea of it.

"But I don't think I can," he continued, watching her face fall and her gaze drop to the ground. "I think being back together for this short time has just confused things between us. Pretending to be married, raising Luna together… I worry that this situation will make us think we're feeling things again when we really aren't."

Mason thought he was saying the right things, but the look that formed on Scarlet's face told him otherwise.

She put her hand back on his chest. "So when I feel your heartbeat speed up when I touch you… I'm not really feeling that?"

"Well, I…"

Scarlet's hand traveled down his stomach and located the desire he'd tried hard to hide from her. "And this?" she asked. "Am I imagining that, too?"

"No." There was no sense in arguing that. "I've never stopped wanting you, Scarlet. Our divorce has never been about that. It's been—"

"Stop," Scarlet said. "Stop saying things that you and I both know don't really mean anything. You're letting your mind get in the way of how your body feels. I know what it wants. And I know what I want. At least for tonight. Forget about the divorce and what you should or shouldn't do right now. Tonight, show me how you feel about me, Mason, and kiss me."

Scarlet's palm pressed hard into the fly of his suit pants, and what little restraint he had left vanished. Lunging forward, he captured her face in his hands and pinned her body back against the side of the car. The night before, their kiss had been almost like that of teenagers, getting a feel for new territory. Tonight, they were old lovers reunited.

The way her tongue grazed along his…the way her back arched and pressed into his body…the way she gave herself to him in every way he demanded… That was like coming home. His whole body responded to the familiar stimuli, his nerves lighting up and demanding more.

And if he was honest with himself, he wanted more. He wanted everything he'd missed out on since their relationship disintegrated in his hands. If he set aside all the reasons why they couldn't be together, just for tonight, he wouldn't be able to stop from claiming her as his own. But he didn't want to do it in a restaurant parking lot with Luna asleep a foot away. As much as he hated to, he pulled away, giving himself some distance and perspective. It was possible that the moment would pass and he wouldn't get this opportunity again, but it didn't matter.

Scarlet looked up at him with the sleepy, passionate eyes that he recognized from their years together. She wasn't finished with him. Not even close. "Now take me home, put Luna to bed, and let's finish this properly."

Scarlet was thankful that Luna slept like a rock. They carried her inside, changed her into a clean diaper and pajamas, and put her down in her crib without her so much as squirming or making a cry of complaint.

They shut the door of the nursery and found themselves standing at the bottom of the staircase together.

It was now or never.

She might regret this later, but right now she didn't care. She couldn't remember the last time she'd made love to Mason. Things had been so strained. Even if this was the one and only time they gave in to their desires for each other, she was okay with that. But she was going to burn tonight into her memories forever.

Reaching out to him, she took his hand and led him upstairs. In the bedroom they'd once shared, she walked over to the wall of windows and opened them up to let the sea air and night breezes blow through. Outside, the sky was as inky black as the sea with the moonlight highlighting the crest of the waves as they washed ashore. In the distance, the lights of ships were visible as they disappeared into the horizon.

As she watched the water, she felt the heat of Mason's body come up behind her and envelop her. She leaned back against him, letting him snake his arms around her waist and pull her close. Scarlet had always loved the feel of being in Mason's arms. She'd never been the daintiest or most graceful of women—at five-ten and with a solid build that inevitably weighed more than anticipated on the scales, she'd been envious of the petite women with their tiny shoes, tiny clothes... Any man could lift them into his arms and carry them into the bedroom to make love to them.

That wasn't ever the case with Scarlet. At least before she met Mason. He was six-one with a large, strong build, and when he'd held her, he'd made her feel feminine and delicate for the first time. And on their wedding night, he had carried her over the threshold of their home, something she never thought would happen to her.

"I've missed this," he said as he swept her hair

over one shoulder to expose the line of her neck. "I've missed touching you. Kissing you."

Scarlet closed her eyes to fully experience every sensation as his mouth ran from her shoulder up to the hollow behind her ear. It felt like sparks flickering across her skin, the heat making her shiver despite the warm night air. She couldn't remember how long it had been since he touched her like this, but she wanted to remember this moment for as long as she could.

Mason slipped the flimsy straps of her top off her shoulders along with her bra straps. She held her breath in her lungs as she waited for his touch. Her breasts ached to be held again.

Mason didn't disappoint. He unsnapped her bra and let it fall to the floor along with the top, which slipped over her hips and gathered at her feet. His large hands immediately covered her bare breasts, his warm touch making her nipples pebble against his palms.

The air rushed out of her lungs on a pleasurable sigh. She melted into him, rolling her head back over his shoulder and exposing her throat and chest for Mason to do as he pleased. He pinched and teased at her rippled flesh, knowing just how to ride the line between pleasure and pain and drawing a cry from the back of her throat.

As he held one breast firmly in his left hand, Mason's right hand strayed down her soft belly to the waistband of her skirt. He slipped beneath it, moving aside her panties to find her silky center with his fingertips.

Scarlet gasped and arched into his hand. "Mason..." she whispered.

"It's been too long," he said. "A woman like you isn't meant to go without a man's touch. You're already ready for me. I guess that means we can save a long night of foreplay for another day."

A ping of awareness went off in Scarlet's brain. Did tonight mean more than she thought it did? It didn't sound as though he was working under the premise of one night for old times' sake.

Did it matter? Not right now. She would deal with the fallout in the morning. She wasn't about to put on the brakes while he was stroking her center so expertly. He had been right about one thing—she was ready for him. He'd barely touched her and she was aching to have him. One stroke across her sensitive parts had put her on the edge. If he wanted to, he could send her over with the flick of his wrist.

And he knew it.

"Are you close?" he asked. "I want to hear you come apart for me. That sound has haunted my dreams these last few months without you in my bed. Let me hear it again. I thought I never would."

Scarlet barely had a choice in the matter. He placed a breathy kiss against her neck and stroked her hard and fast. In half a heartbeat, she found herself trembling in his arms.

"Yes," he coaxed as the pleasure washed over her like the crashing waves down below.

Suddenly, her knees were like butter, her throat was raw from her cries, and if not for Mason's support, she'd be pooled on the floor with her clothes. He held her tight through the whole thing, finally walking her backward to the bed. She didn't have enough energy to do anything other than exactly what he guided her to do.

With the backs of her calves pressed against the bed, she fell onto the mattress. Mason moved quickly to her hip, where he located the zipper to her skirt and slid it down. She lifted her pelvis just high enough for him to pull the skirt and her panties down the length of her legs.

Scarlet expected him to join her on the bed, but instead he simply stood there, admiring her. "What is it?" she asked.

"You're just so beautiful," he said.

She squirmed under his scrutiny. "I look the same as I ever have."

"Exactly. You were beautiful then and you're beautiful now." He started unbuttoning his shirt with his eyes still fixed on her naked body. "I'd tried to convince myself that you weren't as sexy as I remembered. That I'd embellished your appeal in my mind. But I was wrong. You're even more alluring than you were in my memories."

Mason tugged his shirt off and threw it aside. Scarlet tried not to stare too much at his broad chest and strongly carved arms, but she couldn't help it. It was her favorite part of him. Years of paddling his surfboard out into the sea had created a hard, defined body. She could even remember the first time she'd seen him walk up onto the beach with his wet suit peeled down to his waist. Her tongue had suddenly become so large in her mouth that she could barely speak when he said hello to her.

The years had added a few pounds and a manly scattering of chest hair, but she liked it. She was especially happy to see his trousers declaring he felt the same way about her. Scarlet licked her lips in anticipation as Mason unfastened his belt and slipped out of his pants.

She pushed herself into a seated position and slid farther back across the bed. As she inched away, Mason moved forward until his large body was hovering over her own. The heat of his skin so near to her own chased away the chill of the sea air. It made her want to curl against him. Instead, she lay back and wrapped her arms around his neck to pull him into a kiss.

Mason propped on his elbows and settled against her body as his lips touched hers. The heat of his skin pressed against hers sent a chill through her and a wave of goose bumps in its wake. She couldn't get enough of him—his kiss, his touch, his scent.

Scarlet had tried to be strong as she watched their marriage fall apart—as Mason started sleeping in the guest room before finally moving out entirely. He had pulled away from her and taken with him everything that she loved, everything that was important in her life. Now, as she held everything precious to her in her arms and cradled him between her thighs, she wasn't sure whether to hold on tighter so she wouldn't lose him again, or to cling to her heart instead. She could only choose one.

Tonight could be just tonight. Or it could be a few days, a few weeks of enjoying the physical side of their relationship while they could. There was no way to know. Once Jay passed, everything would change, and Scarlet wasn't sure how she wanted things to end. Did she dare hope to keep Mason and Luna in her life? To hope, only to lose them both, was something she wasn't sure she could go through again.

"Get out of your head," Mason whispered in her ear.

He'd caught her overthinking this. It was the risk of giving herself to someone who knew her almost better than she knew herself. Before she could respond, he pressed into her. As his firm heat pushed farther inside of her, setting off sparks of pleasure through her body, all the thoughts and worries disappeared. This moment, right here, was all she needed to focus on. She needed to enjoy it. Cherish it.

Scarlet pulled her knees up to cradle his hips and draw him deeper inside. He groaned and swore softly against the bare skin of her shoulder before nipping gently at it. She gasped and arched her back, urging him on.

Mason thrust into her, apparently setting aside any thoughts of a slow, romantic seduction as his need took over everything else. She raised her hips to meet his every advance, feeling the familiar tension in his body increase even as her own release built up inside her again.

"Are you going to come for me again?" he asked in a rough voice that betrayed how close he was. "Please say yes. I need to hear it again." Mason slipped his hand between them to stroke her center.

"Yes," she gasped. "I…" was all she managed to get out before Mason thrust hard inside of her and she came apart. Like glass shattering, the pleasure shot through her in every direction and then rained down all over her body.

Through her own cries of passion, she heard Mason's own low groan as he stiffened and poured into her. Rolling to his side, he collapsed onto the bed beside her.

After a few moments of rushed breath and racing heartbeats, the room grew awkwardly quiet. Now that the wave of passion had faded, they seemed to be at a loss for words. She wasn't sure what to do. Normally, she would've curled against him and fallen asleep. That felt a bit too comfortable, too familiar for where they found themselves now. That was the risky part of falling back in bed with an old lover—moving too far, too fast. She didn't want to do that and ruin the moment, along with any chance of future moments.

But the mood had probably already soured. Scarlet could almost feel the tension, as if a cloud of regret was settling down over them both. It had come even more quickly than she ever anticipated.

The loud cry of Luna echoing from downstairs provided her the out she desperately needed. "I'll get her," she said. Rolling out of bed, she pulled her robe out of the closet and slipped it on before disappearing from the room.

As though things weren't already complicated enough without the reminder of why they were really together.

Six

Mason awoke the next morning back on the futon in Scarlet's studio. She hadn't asked him to leave the night before, but the speed at which she fled their bed had made it obvious that she had some regrets over what had happened. He had a few of his own, although they hadn't been enough to stop him from sleeping with her again.

While she had been downstairs with Luna, he'd gathered up his clothes and carried them back to the studio with him. She hadn't come looking for him. He hadn't even heard her come back upstairs. Instead, he was awakened by sunlight and the sound of Luna squealing with laughter.

He knew he needed to go downstairs and talk to Scarlet about what happened. They were adults. Married adults at that. He was supposed to be able to tell her anything, but he was dragging his feet because he wasn't sure what kind of conversation he wanted to have with her.

Mason opted for a shower instead to gather his thoughts first. As he stepped into the streams of steamy water, he was reminded of the warm oblivion he'd found in Scarlet the night before. He'd missed it. That much had been obvious. Their physical relationship had been passionate and nearly overwhelming. That hadn't changed even as their circumstances had. But was it the right thing for both of them? Especially for Scarlet?

Leaving her had been hard. Walking out of their home with luggage in his hands had been one of the most difficult things he'd ever done. He never thought he and Scarlet would divorce, much less that he would be the initiator. The only thing that had propelled his concrete-filled shoes down the driveway to his car was the knowledge that this was the best thing for her. She didn't believe that, but it was true.

They'd both survived the separation. Like riding out a rough withdrawal, they'd made it through to the other side only to backslide. Now he had to decide if he was going to continue to indulge in something he knew he shouldn't, or if he was going to put himself through the hell of getting over her a second time.

If he'd actually gotten over her the first time.

He'd fallen into her bed so quickly it made him think otherwise.

Once he was dressed and had made it downstairs, he found Scarlet in the nursery painting again. She was back on the ladder in one of his old T-shirts she'd long ago claimed and a pair of yoga pants smeared in blue and orange paint. Luna was lying on the baby jungle activity mat on the floor, alternating between laughing and chewing on a toy tiger that hung from the bar overhead.

"Good morning," Scarlet said without turning away from her work. Her voice was frustratingly neutral, giving him no clue to which outcome she was hoping for today.

"Morning," he replied with the same noncommittal voice. "It's looking great."

"Thanks. I should have it done today or tomorrow depending on how much Lulu lets me work."

An idea came to Mason's mind. "I was actually thinking of taking her to see Jay today before I went into the office. That would give you a couple hours to work uninterrupted." *And give us some time apart to think.* "Then Carroll should be back soon, right?"

Scarlet set down the brush and nodded. "That's what she said, but I told her that if she's still feeling bad she should stay with her sister. She may not be contagious, but she'll be miserable and that's not good either. I'm not worried about it, although you taking Luna to see Jay is a great idea. She's fed and dressed for the day. You'll just need to pack a diaper bag to take with you. There's a bottle made up in the fridge."

Mason hadn't thought that far ahead. Running an errand with a baby in tow was a completely different scenario. It was something he'd managed to stay ignorant of when they had Evan. Scarlet had stayed home with him while he was at work. This time, it would be just him and Luna. He had to remember the diapers, the wipes, the toys and the food. He had to know how to set up the stroller and how to change a diaper without it sliding right off.

Carroll would be there to help in the future, but he needed to know these things, too, if he was going to be a single father. The idea was terrifying. He owned and ran a major retail chain he'd started from a cart on the beach. He could handle any crisis, and yet this tiny human threw him for a loop. He wouldn't tell his brother or Scarlet or anyone else how he felt, but it was true.

"Thank you," he muttered, turning in search

of the diaper bag she'd referenced. After a moment of searching in vain, he heard the creak of the ladder as Scarlet climbed down.

She went straight to the bag, lifting it over onto the changing table. She grabbed a handful of diapers and stuffed them inside the bag. "This is more than you'll need, but better safe than sorry. There's already wipes in here and a change of clothing in case of disaster."

"Disaster?" Mason frowned.

"Yes, either she spits up all over herself or she has a massive diaper malfunction."

"Oh," he said with wide eyes. Those were possibilities that hadn't even crossed his mind.

"There's a container of Cheerios left over from last night and, like I said, a bottle in the fridge."

Mason lifted the bag. "Thank you."

Looking up, he noticed that Scarlet was making eye contact with him for the first time since the night before. "You'll be fine. You'll learn all this soon enough."

He was glad she had confidence in him. He

wasn't so sure. Before he forgot, he grabbed the bottle from the refrigerator and tucked it into the diaper bag. He slung it over his shoulder and picked Luna up off the floor. "Thanks, Scarlet." The words felt odd in his mouth. There was a time when he never said her name. Scarlet's name was "babe." But despite last night, it didn't seem appropriate. Things were...unresolved at best.

"Say hello to Jay for me," she said before picking up a brush and returning to the mural.

"Will do." Mason and Luna headed out the door and loaded into the car. Since the funeral, Jay had been moved from the hospital to a hospice care facility. Some terminal patients returned home, but with Rachel gone and Luna with Mason, there was no point. The nursing facility was closer to Malibu, so they were there in less than twenty minutes.

After they signed in, they were directed to the hallway where Jay was now staying. He readjusted Luna on his hip and knocked at the door.

"Come in," his brother's voice responded. At

least it sounded like a version of his brother's voice. It was weak and shakier than he'd ever heard it before.

Mason pushed open the door and stepped in. "You've got a very small visitor, Daddy."

Jay's eyes lit up the moment his gaze fell on Luna. "Hello, my beautiful girl," he said, reaching out to hold her.

Luna squealed with a wide grin and reached for Jay. Mason gently settled her into Jay's arms, making sure she wasn't pulling on any of his IVs or monitoring wires. Once he was certain she was steady, he sat in the guest chair and gave them a moment together. They had precious few left.

"Thank you for bringing her by," Jay said after a couple of minutes chatting with her and getting big hugs. "She's the best medicine I've received in days."

"How are you feeling?" Mason asked.

"Truthfully?" he asked with a heavy sigh. "Like I'm about to die. But I've felt like this for several weeks now. Now that we've stopped treatment, I almost feel better. The chemo was so hard on my system. But even so, I know I'm counting down the hours."

Mason wanted to argue with his brother and tell him that negative talk wouldn't help matters, but he held his tongue. They were past the point of trying to be ridiculously positive. Cancer had won the war and they both knew it.

"How have things been with you and Scarlet lately?"

Mason sat bolt upright in his seat, an undisguised look of panic on his face. "What? What do you mean?"

"I mean how has it been for you two having Luna around? You've spent most of your marriage just the two of you. Suddenly having a baby in the house has to be different. Or even difficult, considering how long you two struggled to start a family."

Mason sighed in relief and shook his head. "It's an adjustment, I won't lie. We brought Carroll over, but she's had the flu the last few days, so we've been on our own. Scarlet has adapted to having a baby in the home faster than I have, of course—she was the one home with Evan while I was at work."

"You seem to be doing fine. Luna wasn't screaming when you came in, so she must like you."

Mason chuckled softly. "Well, that's just because she's a mellow baby and we've had her less than a week. I don't know how I'm going to handle the idea of every week from here on out. School, boys, makeup, broken hearts..."

Jay looked at his daughter as she snuggled against his chest. "You'll handle it like every other father handles it. You learn. You make mistakes. You get better. As long as she grows up to be a relatively functional member of society, you've done your job."

"You make it sound deceptively simple."

"It is that simple," Jay said. "And that hard. And that wonderful. You and Scarlet will do just fine.

I have all the faith in the world that the two of you will be good parents. You might even be better at it than Rachel and I would've been because you two have wanted a child for so many years."

Mason's gaze dropped to the floor. He couldn't look his brother in the eye and not tip him off that something was wrong. Lying to Jay about the divorce had seemed like a good idea at the time. Now, facing him, it felt awful. Mason's only consolation was knowing that no matter what happened between him and Scarlet, Luna would be as well cared for as humanly possible. But he still couldn't tell Jay the truth. He couldn't bring back Rachel or cure his brother's cancer, but he could ease Jay's worries about Luna and her future.

So he would keep his damn mouth shut.

Scarlet and Luna were sitting on the beach together the following afternoon when her cell phone rang. She picked it up, spying her manager April's number on the screen.

ANDREA LAURENCE 137

"Don't eat the sand," she said to Luna as she answered the call.

"I'll try," April replied.

"Very funny." Scarlet wiped the sand off Luna's face and handed her the little plastic shovel to play with instead.

"I'm calling to be polite and warn you that I'm on my way to your place. I hate to just arrive unannounced."

Scarlet frowned at the ocean. "Thanks for the heads-up. Why are you coming by again?"

"Have you forgotten what day it is?"

She ran through a dozen options in her brain without landing on something relevant. "Thursday?"

"It's *Wednesday*. And no, that's not why I'm coming. I'm coming to pick up the Maui mural. You said you'd have it done by today. I've got to get it copied and crated to ship. It's done, right?"

"Yes, it's done." Thankfully, Scarlet had finished it up the day before as she attempted to avoid Mason when he got home from his visit with Jay. There might still be a couple tacky spots where it wasn't fully dry, but it was done. She'd set some fans up the night before to help it along.

"Good. I'll see you in ten."

The phone went dead. With a sigh, Scarlet stood up and dusted the sand off her shorts. "We've got to go back inside, Lulu. Auntie April is on her way to get our whale picture for Mr. Bishop."

Luna stuck out her bottom lip and gave a yelp of displeasure as Scarlet picked her up off the beach towel. Settling the baby on her hip, she tossed the shovel into the bucket and picked up the towel with a shake. Back inside the house, she put Luna into her playpen. There, she immediately forgot about the beach and was content to find some of her favorite toys. With Luna happy, Scarlet went upstairs to check on the painting.

All things considered, it might just be one of her favorite pieces. It would be perfect for the Mau Loa Maui. She'd toured the hotel a few months back when she was desperate for a reason to get out of the house for a few days. Things at home had reached a fever pitch with Mason and she thought a break would help things between them.

It hadn't.

But the trip hadn't been completely in vain. The owner of the hotel, Kal Bishop, had given her the freedom to paint whatever she wanted to. Seeing the space where the painting would hang in the hotel helped her visualize what kind of piece to create and what scale would fit it.

It was also an inspiring trip. Seeing the humpback whales breaching just off the shore of the hotel had made it easy to decide what to feature. In the late winter and early spring months, the humpback whales traveled to the warm Hawaiian waters to mate and give birth to their calves. Typically, the mother and calf would be joined by a male escort who was there to protect them and hopefully get the chance to be the next calf's father. That was why she'd chosen to paint a large-scale image of three humpback whales—the mother, the calf and the escort.

As Scarlet was picking up the first panel to carry it downstairs, she heard the doorbell ring. She hauled it to the first floor and left it leaning against the wall to open the door.

April was standing there, looking smart in her linen suit and Gucci sunglasses. "You're not lying to me, right?" she asked without saying hello. "The painting is finished?"

"Finished, yes. Completely dry and ready to ship, perhaps not. You may want to wait a day or two before you get it photographed and scanned for the catalogs and prints. Then it should be dry enough to wrap it and box it up."

"I'll take it." April pushed into the door and turned to inspect the panel beside her.

Her critical eye had always been helpful to Scarlet. Sometimes she didn't know when a painting was truly finished. Usually "done" was determined by when April snatched it from her hands.

"What's it called?" she asked.

"New Life in Maui," Scarlet said.

"I could use a new life in Maui," April quipped. "There's three pieces?"

"Yes."

"I'll go lay down the seats of my Lexus."

Scarlet carried down the other two panels and they were able to set them in the back of April's SUV without any wet-paint disasters. She expected April to take off, but instead she shut the trunk and followed Scarlet back into the house.

"Is it wine o'clock yet?"

Scarlet shrugged. "I've got a bottle of chardonnay in the chiller even if it isn't."

"Perfect."

April poured herself a glass while Scarlet checked on Luna. She looked like she was ready for her afternoon nap. After picking her up out of the playpen, she carried her into the nursery. Just as she got Luna settled in, she heard April's loud voice behind her.

"What the hell is that?" she shrieked.

"Shh!" Scarlet hissed before turning back to check on Luna. She looked a little surprised, with wide eyes, but after a moment of her little music box playing, she eventually closed her eyes again. Having dodged that bullet, Scarlet scooted April out of the room and shut the door behind her.

"I'm waiting," April said in a quiet yet annoyed tone.

Scarlet took her by the arm and led her over to the living room, where they sat on the couch. "It's just something I painted for Luna," she said at last.

"Luna, the little girl you were keeping your distance from? Luna, the baby that your soon-to-be ex-husband has custody of? Luna, the adorable chubby-cheeked child that has obviously wormed her way into your heart?"

That was a lot to take in all at once, but Scarlet listened and finally nodded. Thankfully, Mason was at the office and not around to hear all that. "Yes," she vocalized.

"Care to tell me what's changed since the last time I saw you?"

Not really. But Scarlet knew she needed someone to talk to. Things had gotten a little complicated lately. Wishing she had a glass of wine of her own but not wanting to drink while Luna was in her care, she took a deep breath and started at the beginning. She began with the first few awkward days, the late-night kiss, the nanny's illness and finally falling back into bed with Mason. The more she spoke, the more April's eyes seemed to widen. "And now we're avoiding one another," she said, finishing off her sordid tale.

"Uh-huh," April replied before taking a large sip of her wine. "It's hard to believe you've lived a life that dramatic and yet still managed to paint a huge panel piece and a mural."

"When I wanted to avoid Mason, I worked."

"Remind me to thank him later."

"Don't thank him just yet. I don't know that he deserves it."

"Why? Was the sex…?" April tilted her hand side to side in a "so-so" gesture.

"No! It was…well, it was just like it was before.

Even more like it was early in our relationship. I'm just worried."

"About what?"

Scarlet sighed. "About everything. Mason walked away from me and bought that place in the Hills. Then the next thing I know, he's moving back in and kissing me. He makes love to me, and then he avoids me. Was I just a convenient outlet for pent-up sexual energy or did it mean something more to him? I don't know what to think of all of this. It's certainly not the fairy-tale reunion you're hoping for, I'm sorry to say."

April considered her words thoughtfully for a moment. "Well, there might be more to his motives than just sex or rekindling your romance. Do you think he's trying to win you back just so Luna will have a mother? Or more to the point, so he doesn't have to be a single father?"

Scarlet blinked a few times. She hadn't considered that before. He'd been the one pushing the divorce from day one. She'd never wanted it, but he wouldn't listen to her, as usual. This sudden turnaround once Luna entered the picture could be seen as suspicious. Did he really want *her* back or was he just unwilling to face his unexpected and scary future all alone?

"I don't know," Scarlet admitted. "But I do know he hasn't mentioned anything about a future together or calling off the divorce. Our night together felt very in the moment. As far as I know, all this ends once Jay is gone, since it's all for his benefit."

"Sleeping with you wasn't for Jay's benefit."

"True. That might've just been an unintended side effect of our arrangement. But he's acted weird since then. I think he regrets it."

"And do you regret it?"

More than ever, Scarlet wished that April had loaded up those panels and taken them to the shop instead of loitering around and digging into her personal business. These weren't easy answers. She wasn't about to let this go, though.

"I do and I don't. I regret that it complicated matters between us and strained what little friendship we had left. But at the same time, it was so amazing to be in his arms again. I've missed him. I wouldn't admit that to anyone but you, but I have. This whole scenario—pretending to be a family, living together again, having a baby to care for, making love—it has me all turned around. I don't know whether I'm coming or going anymore."

"Well, for your sake," April said, "I hope you're coming, or it's hardly worth the trouble."

"April!"

Her manager laughed and drained the last of her wine. "I kid, I kid. Just trying to keep things light. There's entirely too much drama in your life. Of course, you're an artist. You thrive on drama."

Scarlet wrinkled her nose. She hated drama. She wasn't a van Gogh out there pining for her lost love and painting her feelings. She painted what she saw. And yet, as an artist, she knew how her moods could affect her work. The mural in Luna's room had been a joyful piece because of how she felt painting it. So maybe April was onto something. "Whatever you say, manager lady."

"Can I get that recorded so I can hear it when you're being contrary or moody with me? No? Okay, fine." April set her wineglass down on the table and stood up. "I'm going to get those panels ready to go, and then I'm heading up to San Francisco to oversee the last-minute details of the gallery opening. All this drama isn't going to interfere with that, is it?"

"I don't think so." The only thing she could envision being an issue was if Jay were to pass, but there was no way of knowing when that would happen. April should know that was a possibility, so there was no reason to mention it to her and start her worrying unnecessarily.

"Well, I hope not. Opening your gallery without you there is kind of pointless. We've gotten over a hundred and fifty RSVPs from art connoisseurs in the area. They're coming to meet you and admire your work. I intend to sell more than a few of your pieces that night and I need you there to shake their hands and talk up your work. Got it?"

Scarlet sighed. This was hardly her first gallery opening. She knew how it would work. Mingle, sip wine, smile and sell herself to the art-appreciating public. Normally, it didn't bother her. She much preferred days spent painting in dirty overalls with her hair in a ponytail, but dressing up every now and then to sell her work made those other days possible. "I'll be there with bells on."

"That's what I want to hear. My assistant will email you your itinerary and hotel information. I'll see you up there. Oh, and when you're done with that mural—" she gestured toward the nursery "—let me know. I'll send someone over here to photograph it and get it cataloged. I don't want any Scarlet Spencer originals floating around without my knowledge. It all goes into the portfolio."

"It's just a mural for Luna," Scarlet argued.

"If I had painted it, sure. But when an internationally recognized wildlife artist paints a giant mural of her subject of choice, it's not just decoration in a baby's room any longer. You should've opted for teddy bears if you didn't want me putting prints into production. Sorry."

Scarlet got up and walked April to the door. "Okay. I'll see you next weekend."

"All right. Keep me posted on how things are going with the ex. If necessary, we can book a second ticket and you can bring him with you."

Scarlet flinched. "Bring Mason with me to the opening?"

"Why not?" April asked. "If you two are still together publicly, wouldn't you want him to come? And even more importantly, don't you think some time alone with him could help you figure out what he really wants from you?"

She had a point, Scarlet had to admit. "I'll keep that in mind," she said. "We'll have to stop avoiding each other first."

April just smiled and slung her purse over her shoulder. "You two can't avoid each other for long. You've got more chemistry than a sophomore in high school."

Seven

Scarlet was at the store and Luna was taking a nap, since she'd been a little fussy all afternoon. Mason was finally getting more comfortable having the baby with no one else around, but he was certainly feeling more confident with Luna asleep. Carroll was planning on coming back tonight after several days of misery on her sister's couch, so soon neither he nor Scarlet would have to watch Luna every second of the day.

That was good. He had a company to run and Scarlet was headed to San Francisco soon to open her latest gallery. Neither of them had really had the chance to adapt their lives to the addition of a baby. If Scarlet could've gotten pregnant or they were going through the adoption process, they would've had months to plan and prepare before a child arrived. Luna was simply there one day. Carroll had been convenient to slip into their lives, but adjustments still needed to be made.

Especially once he was on his own without Scarlet.

She knew exactly what to do when it came to handling babies, while he was completely clueless. He wasn't entirely sure how she got so comfortable around them, but he admired her for it. A lot of it just seemed like a mother's instinct.

Mason was about to consider a nap of his own when he heard a sudden, angry wail coming from Luna's nursery. He didn't know much, but he was pretty certain that something was wrong. It didn't sound like her usual cry for food or a change of diaper. He opened the door to the nursery and found that she had gone from fussy to a complete meltdown.

She was standing in the crib, gripping the bars with her tiny fists. Her face was bright red with both tears and a stream of snot running down her face. He picked her up and held her close, her cheek brushing across his. He nearly flinched from the contact because her skin was burning up with fever.

Mason tried not to panic. Babies got sick. That was just what happened. But he didn't know exactly what to do. At the same time, he didn't want to call for help either. If he was going to raise Luna, he needed to be able to figure this out on his own.

He carried her over to the changing table and opened the drawers until he found one filled with creams, medicines and something that looked like a weird flashlight. Picking it up, he realized it was actually an in-ear thermometer. He tested it on himself, then carefully pressed it to Luna's ear.

After a few seconds, it beeped and the screen read 100.9 degrees. It was higher than his, but he wasn't sure how high was too high for her age. He carried her into the kitchen to look up the pediatrician's phone number where they'd posted it on the refrigerator for Carroll. He was fishing his phone out of his pocket while holding a squirming and still screaming Luna when Scarlet came in through the garage with her hands full of grocery bags.

Her dark brown eyes widened as she took in the scene in the kitchen. "What's wrong?" she asked and placed the groceries on the ground.

He'd never been so happy to see Scarlet in his life. He didn't want to call for help, but if she was here, he could at least watch and learn. "She woke up from her nap with a fever and a runny nose. I was about to call the pediatrician to see if we need to take her in or not."

"Did you take her temperature?"

"Yes," Mason said, thankful he'd at least gotten the first step right. "Yes, it's just under 101."

"That's good. Any higher can be dangerous. Did you give her some baby Motrin?"

He shook his head. "Not yet. Is that what you give babies for fever?"

Scarlet nodded. "It's in the guest bathroom cabinet. I'll go get it. That should help bring down her fever, and if we can't get her to the doctor until tomorrow, she'll at least be more comfortable."

"How do we get her to swallow a pill?" Mason asked, trailing behind her.

"It's a liquid." She pulled the box from the bathroom and showed him the bottle with the dropper. "She won't take pills until she's quite a bit older."

Mason felt both stupid and relieved at the same time. He remembered trying to get the family cat to take a pill once and it had been a nightmare. He couldn't imagine doing that to an infant. He had so much to learn; it was more intimidating than college. No matter how this new family had come about, Mason wanted to do a good job. He didn't want Luna to cry for her nanny when she was hurt or sick. He wanted her to want him, like she would her real daddy. That meant knowing how to handle these kinds of situations, and he was starting from the very bottom.

He held Luna as Scarlet filled the dropper and squirted it into Luna's open mouth. The sudden arrival startled her out of crying for a moment as she swallowed the medicine. Her bottom lip pouted out—he imagined the flavor wasn't so great—and then she began to cry again.

"What now?"

"I think we make her a cool bottle of electrolyte water so she doesn't get dehydrated and I'll call the doctor."

"Okay." Mason rocked Luna back and forth on the balls of his feet while Scarlet disappeared into the kitchen to make the call he'd tried to make earlier. By the time she'd gotten off the phone, Luna had calmed down a little, so he carried her into the living room and sat down in a recliner. He rocked back and forth, petting her back and trying to soothe her as much as he could. Eventually, her cries faded to a fussy sort of whining that was much easier to take.

He didn't like this at all. Mason was the CEO of his own company. He was used to being able to handle any situation. He snapped his fingers and a dozen people ran out of the room to make things happen. There was nothing he could do to fix this. They could give her medicine and make her comfortable, but an illness usually had to run its course. He didn't like seeing Luna miserable, and this was just a fever. He couldn't imagine her being seriously ill or hospitalized.

Scarlet came into the room with a bottle. "The nurse said that the fever is low enough not to bring her in tonight. At this point, they can't be sure if it's just a cold or if Carroll gave her the flu. They said to keep an eye on things and bring her in tomorrow morning. If she develops any other flu symptoms, they can give her the medication for that."

Mason was relieved they didn't think it was serious, but their response still left him with questions. "So what can we do for now? She's pretty miserable."

"Give her this for a start," she said, handing over the bottle of water. "If she'll drink it. The medicine should kick in pretty soon and her fever will go down. We can give her a cool bath. Hold her a lot. Basically, just love on her and keep her from getting overheated."

Mason offered the bottle to Luna and she took it, sniffling sadly as she suckled on it. "How do you know all this stuff?" he asked her when Luna appeared to be settled for the moment. "You were an only child. You weren't raised around any other kids, were you?"

"No. But when we found out we were getting Evan, I read a lot so I'd be prepared on day one. I was so worried I was going to screw something up and they'd take him away."

Mason's jaw tightened. Her worst fears had been realized through no fault of her own and he hated that, but it was another scenario he had no control over. Child-rearing was far more stress-ful than business any day. "I don't know how I'm going to manage this on my own."

Scarlet sat back on the couch and looked at him. "You're doing just fine."

"Because you came home just in time."

"No," she insisted with a shake of her head. "You checked her temperature and you were about to call the doctor. They would've told you what to do even if you weren't sure. You could've handled this. You're going to be a great father. I always thought you would be."

He wasn't so sure of that, but he knew she was destined to be a great mother. Part of him wanted her to be that mother to Luna, but he wouldn't force that on her. If she wanted her own children, she deserved that.

"I remember you sitting in that same chair hold-ing Evan not long after he came to us," she con-tinued. "I was so enamored with him I'd hardly put him down for a week, but I was desperate for a shower. You took him while I washed my hair, and when I came downstairs, the two of you were just like this."

Mason remembered that day. He'd been terrified by the idea of holding such a small baby, but he'd done just fine. At least for fifteen minutes or so. Evan slept most of the time, so it hadn't been as much of a challenge as today had been. "You had the magic touch with Evan. The minute you picked him up, he'd stop crying."

"It's not magic," Scarlet said. "It's love and trust. The baby bonds with you and you with it. When they know that you'll do whatever it takes to keep them safe and happy, that's where they want to be. Eventually, Evan would've been just as contented with you as he was with me. And the same goes for Luna. You're going to be her whole world and she'll love you more than anyone else on the planet, and you'll feel the same way. When you run across a speed bump, you'll figure it out. That's just parenting. You can't expect to know everything, but you adapt and the baby learns to trust in you."

Mason looked down at Luna, who had let the bottle slip from her lips as she fell asleep, then back up at Scarlet. "I never wanted to do this without you. Whenever I imagined a family, it had you in it."

"Life doesn't always turn out the way you plan," Scarlet said with a sad, distant look in her eye. "You two will be just fine."

Mason watched as she turned and walked back into the kitchen to deal with the groceries and end the conversation. He hoped she was right.

Things had begun to return to normal after a day or two. The new normal, anyway. Carroll was back, Luna was on medication and was feeling better. They were starting to settle into a groove. At least it felt that way.

Scarlet was feeling anything but settled. She felt like the world was tipping on its axis and the scariest part of it all was that she liked it. It was far too easy to return to the life she had with Mason, especially adding the piece of her life she always felt was missing. Having Luna made almost everything fall into place for her. That was what made it frightening. This couldn't possibly be her happily-ever-after, could it? Could the Fates really give her everything she wanted and let her be happy? She just couldn't believe it. There had to be a catch.

She was pretty sure that catch was Mason. She just wasn't sure if he felt the same way about how things were going between them. They hadn't really talked about the night they'd spent together. Both of them had artfully dodged the situation, and with Luna getting sick, it was easy to do it. She wasn't sure where they stood long-term. What she did know was that she wasn't going back into this relationship again just because he was scared to care for Luna alone. That was a recipe for disaster.

He'd walked away from their marriage once because he didn't feel like he could give his best to her. Before she could trust her heart in his hands a second time, she had to know that he was in it for the long haul, no matter what challenges came their way. Those things were inevitable, but they were easier to tackle with someone else than alone. At the same time, she didn't want him coming back just because he was afraid to face those scary things without her help.

When she came home from her office that evening, she found the house quieter than it had been since everyone else moved in. She'd stayed late getting things ready for the grand opening but was still surprised by the stillness.

"Hello?" she called as she stepped through the foyer.

"Hello," Mason's voice answered back.

She followed the sound through the sliding glass doors to the deck. Mason was sitting out there with his laptop and a half-empty bottle of beer. "Where's Luna and Carroll?"

"Luna is down for the night and Carroll is reading in her room, so I came out here to work. You stayed pretty late at the office tonight."

She nodded. She did most of her work at home,

but she did have an office she went into occasionally to handle the business side of her art. Today, it was going over all the plans April had put together, overseeing the shipment of works up to the new gallery, finalizing the catering arrangements and approving the hiring of the employees who would be manning the new location.

"Gallery openings are exciting and wonderful and stressful all at once."

He nodded. She'd watched him go through the same anxiety every time he opened a new surf shop. "Well, grab a glass of wine and join me out here. It's a beautiful night."

That was an excellent suggestion. As a couple before children came into the picture, they'd spent more evenings than she could count out on this deck talking. Over a bottle of wine, they'd catch up on their busy work lives, reconnect emotionally and enjoy the soothing rush of the waves at their back door. She didn't realize how much she'd missed those moments with him until she joined him on the porch with a full glass of merlot.

This was where they'd always had their important talks. Something about the sea and the safety of their deck retreat made it easier to share their feelings. Maybe by the time she'd gotten halfway through this wine, she'd have the nerve to bring up their brief encounter the other night. On an empty stomach, the first two sips were strong, warming her blood and loosening her tongue.

"I'm glad we have this moment together to talk. I feel like things have been so hectic lately."

She nodded, deciding to let him say what was on his mind first. It might make whatever she wanted to discuss moot. "It's been a whirlwind since you and Luna arrived."

"Scarlet, things have really been…nice…since I came back. Being here feels just like before. Sitting on this deck with you, it's like the last year and a half never even happened. I probably shouldn't say this, but I hate my new house."

"Why?" She hadn't been there, of course, but

she had no doubt it was superluxurious. Mason strived for the best in all things. Building in Malibu had been their dream, but his place in the Hills was hardly a shack.

"Because it's not home." He looked around their backyard, which included the Pacific Ocean, and reached out to take her hand. When he leaned in, the spicy scent of his cologne mingled with the sea air and tickled at her nose. "This feels like home."

Scarlet couldn't pull away although she knew she should. She liked the feel of her hand in his. The warmth of his skin enveloped her, and he was right, it did feel like home. It hadn't until he came back. The big house had seemed hollow when she was alone and she'd spent many nights walking around wondering how she could ever fill it.

At the same time, she couldn't shake the worry about his timing. Without Luna, he wouldn't be here saying these things to her. This was still the man who left her, and she had to keep reminding herself of that, especially when he leaned in close and smiled at her this way.

"When I realized Jay was leaving Luna to me, it was like the whole world was collapsing around me. I didn't know what I was going to do. I know moving in on your life and pretending like our breakup never happened wasn't ideal, especially for you, but I don't regret it. Being here, raising Luna together, has shown me a lot about the life we never got to have."

She knew what he meant. Even as they avoided the consequences of the physical relationship, she understood how easily it had happened. Slipping back into their life was so easy. So comfortable. She had to fight not to let herself get carried away by the fantasy they created when it was everything she had ever wanted in her life.

"I'm sorry I couldn't give this to you. I'm sorry that I couldn't keep Evan home where he belonged. All you wanted was to have a family with me, and no matter what I seemed to do, I just made it worse."

"None of it was your fault."

"It feels like my fault. But even if all of that was out of my control, leaving you *was* my fault. I hurt you and I'm sorry for that."

"Thank you," she said, accepting the apology he offered. "I'm sorry for disappearing on you the other night."

"I didn't blame you," Mason said as his thumb brushed over the back of her hand. "We didn't plan that, and I don't think either of us were ready to deal with what it meant, if anything, to ourselves and to each other."

"I think we both needed some comfort and a release after everything that has happened."

He nodded. "It was more than that for me, though. That, more than anything else, really made me feel like I'd come home. This place, this life, making love to you again…it was amazing, Scarlet. And I can't stop thinking about it. Thinking about you."

Scarlet held her breath as she anticipated what he would say next. This whole conversation had been unexpected for her. They'd tried to keep their focus on Luna and the situation, but this was treading into unexpected territory.

"I don't know what to do, honestly. I still feel like letting you start a new life is the best thing for you. But if I'm being totally selfish, I want you back. Not just in my bed, but in my life. I want you in Luna's life. She deserves a mother like you would be. When I see you two together, I know that's the way Rachel and Jay wanted it to be."

The words he was saying sounded nice, but Scarlet still wasn't hearing what she wanted. Yes, he liked being back, but was he more interested in the life they'd make for Luna than just being with her again? He hadn't said that he still loved her. That he wanted to be with her no matter what. That he wanted to call off the divorce proceedings. Just that Luna needed her for a mother.

Things were going well enough now, but it wouldn't always be such smooth sailing. Would he turn and run again if something bad happened, like before? Would their fragile peace be destroyed by the finality of Jay's death? His brother's health was deteriorating day by day and their stability could change with a single phone call.

"What do *you* want, Scarlet?"

The question startled her out of her thoughts. It was a question she wasn't used to answering. Mason was bad about making decisions without consulting her. He always insisted he was acting in her best interests, but sometimes people didn't want what was best for them. They just wanted what they wanted. Now that he was asking, she was afraid to throw caution to the wind and be completely honest with him, or with herself.

"I don't know," she said. "These last few weeks have been a taste of the life I've always dreamed of. But I'm afraid it won't last."

"What do you mean?"

"I mean Luna seems to be the linchpin that's holding our relationship together at the moment. But when Evan was pulled from our lives, things fell apart. What if something happens to her? What if someone in Rachel's family takes you to court for custody and you lose? Or she gets sick. Or in a car accident. I feel like what we have would go into a tailspin without her. That scares me."

"Why do you think that?"

"Because you can't deal with failure, Mason. At the slightest sign that something won't work out for you, you bail. I can't have you bailing on this marriage twice."

Mason frowned at her. "No, I don't."

"When grad school got too hard, you dropped out. When your first big project at your dad's company went south, you decided to quit."

"I did both those things so I could focus on starting my own company. Considering how successful the store chain has become, that was the right choice, don't you agree?"

"And did you leave me to focus on starting your own company? No. You did it because you couldn't stand to live each day with me as a reminder that you'd failed at making me a mother. Maybe leaving so I could start over was how you legitimized the decision in your own mind, but with you, I know you're always going to pull away when things get too difficult. Your father programmed you to succeed at all costs. It's not good or bad, it's just the way you are."

Mason let go of her hand and sat back in his seat for a moment to take in everything she said. After a bit, he sighed and nodded. "I guess I do. I've never thought about it that way. I'm sorry you feel like you can't rely on me."

Scarlet shook her head. "Enough apologies for tonight. I just need you to know that I need someone who will stand and fight for this. For us. No one ever said marriage was easy, and raising a family is even harder. You and I have chemistry, there's no doubt of it. But passion alone isn't enough for me. Staying together is a choice you have to wake up and make every day."

Passion faded; she knew that. And if it did, she was in a very precarious position with Mason and

Luna. Unless he allowed her to legally adopt the baby after Jay died, she had no rights to Luna. Just like with Evan, she wouldn't have a leg to stand on in court if they separated again and battled for custody. Losing another child would destroy her and she wasn't sure she could recover from it a second time while also coping with her marriage finally ending. She was already enamored with her niece. But losing her daughter, if she let it go that far, would be devastating.

"Before I can let myself even consider a future with you and Luna in it, I need to know that I'll be able to count on you, especially when things get hard."

Mason listened patiently to everything she had to say. When she was finished, he reached over and cupped her face in his hand. She couldn't resist closing her eyes, leaning into the warmth of his touch and drawing the scent of his skin into her lungs. He was her weakness, and she knew it. All he had to do was say the right words and she'd believe him because she was desperate to believe.

When she opened her eyes again, he was watching her with a serious expression lining his face. "I'm not going to run this time, Scarlet."

He leaned in and followed his promise with a kiss. Scarlet didn't resist. This was what she wanted, even if she was afraid to want it again. She knew this kiss would lead them upstairs and, eventually, would lead her heart down a path of no return. But even then, she kissed him back with all her heart and soul and could only hope for the best.

Eight

Things were going well. Too well.

Mason wasn't known for being the most optimistic person. Running his own company had taught him to always watch for the other shoe to drop. After his talk with Scarlet the other night, things had made a turn for the better. They seemed to really be giving this a chance. He was actually sleeping in their bedroom again, leaving her studio and the lumpy futon behind. Now he got to fall asleep every night with the scent of Scarlet's shampoo on his pillowcase and the warm curve of her body pressed into his.

He could almost forget that the drama of the last year or so had ever happened. And that was what worried him the most. He was not one to get lulled into complacency. That was when fate would throw a curve ball and hit you squarely upside the head. He just wasn't sure what direction the threat would come from next. Would Scarlet decide that she really did want her own child? Would something else drive them apart? Jay's death? Something with Luna? He didn't know. There was no way to know. That was just life. He just needed to be ready for the eventuality.

When Mason pulled his car into the garage that evening, there were no curve balls in sight. When he stepped inside, he could hear commotion out back and saw that Scarlet, Carroll and Luna were playing in the pool together. He stood for a moment at the window, watching Scarlet and Luna.

Scarlet's dark hair was twisted into a messy knot on the top of her head to keep it dry. She was wearing the red halter bikini he'd chosen for her at one of his shops a few years before. She was bouncing up and down, holding on to a little floaty chair that kept Luna upright in the water. The baby was wearing a hot-pink zebra swimsuit with giant sunglasses that nearly covered half her face. She was happily splashing her hands and giggling as the water went everywhere.

The look on Scarlet's face as she played with her niece was enough to make a man melt. Devotion, wonder, joy, amazement...all of those things and more were wrapped up in the wide smile that crossed her face. She was meant to be a mother. He'd always known that, he just hadn't been sure how to make it happen before Luna came into their lives. He might never be able to provide that opportunity the old-fashioned way, but he'd brought a child into her life nonetheless.

He hoped it was enough.

The smile on his own face faded away as he realized what it had cost his family to make it a reality. It was hard to focus on the happiness, on this second chance they'd been given, when it was costing them both Rachel's and Jay's lives. That was a high price, and not how he ever would've wanted it to happen. And yet, here Luna was, in need of a home just as surely as Scarlet needed a child. It was kismet.

Turning away from the window, he noticed his cell phone beeping at his hip. It needed charging. He opened the nearby drawer in search of a cable and immediately forgot all about his phone. Stashed away there was the finalized copy of their divorce agreement. Scarlet's copy.

At this point, there was no reason not to look it over. His copy was probably on hold with no one to sign for it at his new house. There weren't many surprises. They'd gone back and forth after the mediation to get everything settled between them. When Rachel died, the paperwork had become something he'd hardly given a thought to. He supposed that in the back of his mind he knew his attorney was getting things drawn up and ready to sign, but his lawyer didn't know anything about Luna and how much had changed in the last few weeks.

It could change everything. Or nothing. Mason liked to think they were on the path to reconciliation, but he wasn't naive enough to think that a baby could turn everything around. That oversimplified their situation. Yes, losing Evan had pushed them to the end, but they wouldn't have gotten there if they'd been able to communicate better. If he'd been able to understand what Scarlet really needed, not just what he thought she needed.

And maybe he was just presuming that what she wanted or needed was him. Yes, she'd warmed up to him during their time together, but he couldn't be certain he was the sole cause for the smile that returned to her face. More than anything, Scarlet wanted a baby and she seemed really taken with Luna. When he'd drawn Scarlet into this situation, a part of him had hoped that she would fall for the baby and they could reconcile as a complete family at last. Finally being able to give her what she wanted made him feel like he was less of a failure in their marriage.

What he didn't anticipate was that he would feel like the third wheel in his own marriage. Scarlet seemed more devoted to the baby than she was to him. He had to wonder if it was really their marriage she wanted back, or the baby that would now come with the reconciliation package.

Mason would be the first to admit that he was the one who walked away from the marriage. Scarlet was stubborn enough to stick it out no matter how miserable she was with him. But when he walked away, she didn't try to stop him either. The air of tension in the house had become so thick that there was almost a feeling of relief when he told her he was moving out. That, more than anything, had convinced him he was making the right decision.

Looking down at the paperwork now, he wasn't so sure. Now that Scarlet was back in his bed, he had a taste of the family they'd hoped for. Scarlet might be cautious where the two of them were concerned, but that would change with time. Or it should, but he'd have to stand his ground. That was perhaps the hardest part.

It wasn't that Mason was afraid to work hard. He'd work harder than anyone to achieve what he wanted. But he was also realistic and knew when he was banging his head against a brick wall. If he wasn't going to be successful, it didn't seem like a good use of his time. He'd rather stop and change course than go down with the ship. From the outside, he supposed that might look like quitting when things got tough.

He didn't want to quit on Scarlet. Not again. But did he dare to put his whole heart into this reconciliation when he wasn't certain what the future would hold for them?

Mason was about to stuff the papers back into the drawer when he noticed a handwritten note from her attorney. He knew he shouldn't read it, but when he caught a glimpse of Luna's name in the loopy script, he couldn't stop himself.

Scarlet—here's the draft we agreed to with Mason's attorneys. My advice is to hold off on moving forward with the divorce for now. If the situation changes, we want to make sure that the custody and support arrangements for Luna are included. Hope the adoption attorney I recommended was helpful.

He read the note three times before he stuffed it back in with the other pages. He wasn't entirely sure what the note meant. Did she plan to drag out the divorce long enough that she could take custody from him? Or did the lawyer mean that in the event they decided to divorce anyway, they should include something to address the situation with Luna? He didn't feel like Scarlet was working him, but he could be wrong.

Either way, it didn't sound good, and it didn't sound like the words of an attorney who didn't think the divorce was right around the corner. They were discussing adoption attorneys. Was that Scarlet's idea or just her attorney pushing her to cover her bases in a worst-case scenario?

Mason sighed as an ache of worry started to pool in his gut. That was why you never read anyone else's mail. You learned things you didn't really want or need to know. He shoved the kitchen drawer closed and tried to pretend he'd never read that note.

He tried to tell himself that those papers had been in the works for quite some time. She could've discussed this with her attorney long before they got back together. He knew that at this point, he didn't think he wanted to sign and neither did Scarlet, despite what that paperwork might imply. A lot had changed in the last two weeks. It was too early to decide either way. He wouldn't mention the divorce again until he knew for certain. Then they could either tear it up together or sign together and make a plan to move forward.

Until he knew where he stood, however, Mason was going to tread very carefully. He wanted things to work out with Scarlet, but if they didn't, he needed to be mentally prepared for that. The last time, he spent three days in a bourbon-fueled stupor. He couldn't lose it like that with Luna in his life now. He had to be responsible, do the adult thing. And that meant keeping his heart secured until he knew it was safe.

If safe was even an option.

After Luna went down for the night, Scarlet opted for a bubble bath upstairs. It had been a long time since she'd indulged in something so luxurious, but she needed it. Keeping up with her career and a one-year-old was enough to bring on a Calgon moment. She needed to unwind and relax if she was going to make it through the next week. The trip to San Francisco loomed heavy ahead of her.

As she turned off the water and sank, naked, into the bubbles, she felt her tight muscles instantly start to unwind. Her hair was still on the top of her head from the pool, so she was able to lean back onto the bath pillow and close her eyes.

Scarlet was anxious about the San Francisco opening. She really hadn't had the time to think about it with everything else going on, but she was worried. She wasn't entirely sure why. Maybe it was just the idea of being away from her family that bothered her.

Her family?

That was the first time a thought like that had crossed her mind. While it was easy to think of Mason as her husband—technically, he still was—thinking of the whole household as her family was a big step. She'd developed a sense of attachment to them as a whole. Even Carroll. But especially Luna. She had very quickly become Scarlet's baby girl.

Going to San Francisco meant leaving them all behind. Luna and Carroll would fare fine without her, but she still disliked the idea of going. At least right now when everything was so fragile. Especially with Mason.

Of course, she could always ask him to come with her to the gallery opening. The more she soaked, the more she realized that she wanted that. April had planted the bug in her ear when she picked up that painting and now she couldn't imagine going through such a big night without him. But would he go? She'd never asked him to come with her to these things before because it seemed like such an imposition, and that was when their marriage was okay. They seemed to be in such a delicate place at the moment, especially with Jay clinging to the edge of death a few miles up the road. She wasn't sure if Mason would want to go all the way to San Francisco under the circumstances.

But they both said they were going to try harder this time. Communicate better instead of making presumptions. This was important to her, so she was going to ask. It was possible he wouldn't be able to attend, but she should at least give him that option.

When she got done in the tub, she drained

the water and wrapped herself in a fluffy white towel. She was going to head downstairs to talk to him, but when she went into their bedroom, she found him sitting up in bed with a mountain of pillows behind him. He was wearing his favorite pair of striped cotton pajama pants and faded Pepperdine T-shirt from his college days. He had a pair of reading glasses perched low on his nose to see while he was working on his laptop, looking over the top of them to watch a baseball game on the television. The sound was muted so he didn't disturb Scarlet's bath.

"Hey," she said as she approached the bed.

"Hey." Mason shut the laptop and set it on the comforter beside him. He admired her messy, damp hair and nearly inadequate towel over the tops of his glasses with a small smile curling his lips.

"What's with the glasses?" she asked. He'd never worn glasses in the nine years they were together. It seemed strange for something to change about him without her knowing about it. They hadn't been apart that long, but it was apparently long enough.

Mason slipped the black framed glasses off and put them on top of the laptop. "Yeah, those. My optometrist said I needed to start wearing them when I'm on the computer. Eyestrain."

"Put them back on," Scarlet said.

He complied, modeling the new look for her. They were square black frames that mimicked the lines of his jaw nicely. "What do you think? Can I pull off the sexy nerdy look?"

Scarlet smiled. She actually really liked the glasses on him, even if they did give off a bit of the geeky hipster vibe that clashed with the tanned surfer boy she was used to. "You look…"

"Smarter?"

She shrugged. "Maybe. It's a different look for you. But I like them. How long have you been wearing them?"

"About a month. Since I've never worn glasses before, I keep forgetting to put them on. Now that you know, you can nag me about wearing them."

"I'll add that to the list of other things I nag you about, like wearing sunblock and putting the recycling on the curb."

"Very good." Mason slipped the glasses back off and set them aside. "Did you enjoy your bath? You weren't in there for very long."

"I'm not good at sitting still, even when I try to. I thought of something and I got out to talk to you about it. My opening is Saturday. I was wondering if..." Scarlet hesitated. She didn't know why she was so nervous to ask. Perhaps because Mason hadn't been to any of her other openings. This was a big one, though. Her biggest. And she wanted him to be there with her. Somehow it felt like she was asking a boy to prom instead of asking her husband to support a work event.

"If what?" he asked.

She walked around to his side of the bed and leaned her shoulder against the wall. "If you wanted to come with me."

Mason's brow raised curiously. "Really?"

"Yes. I know I've never asked you to come to any before, and I wasn't sure if you had time to go up to San Francisco with me this trip. This event is a lot bigger than some of the others. I'm more nervous about this one. I think April said the mayor RSVP'd. I understand if you—"

"Of course I will," he interrupted.

Scarlet had been on the verge of accepting his excuses as to why he couldn't make it when she realized he'd actually said yes. "You will?"

He nodded. "I realize I haven't made it to the others, but I thought that was what you wanted, since you never asked me to go. Those openings are so stressful for you and I know what it's like opening one of my new stores. Everything comes together at the very last moment. I figured that I would just be a distraction for you on your big nights."

Scarlet could only shake her head. He wouldn't be a distraction. He would be her saving grace. Just the touch of his hand would keep her ship sailing smoothly on the rough seas. "I always just thought you were too busy. I didn't want to bother you with my work when you already had plenty to worry about, running your own company."

Mason peeled back the blankets and stood up, closing the gap between them and putting his hands reassuringly on her upper arms. His skin was warm against hers, sending a shiver through her body even in the comfortable evening air. "I know I work too much, but don't ever think I won't take time out for what's important. My career isn't any more important than yours is. You've done amazing things and I couldn't be prouder of how far you've come as an artist since you first walked into my little shop to sell your paintings. All you have to do is ask me and I'm there."

Scarlet looked up into his sea-blue eyes and knew he meant what he said. Maybe she was wrong about all of this. She'd worried that their physical draw was nothing more than a comfortable distraction from their grief of losing Rachel and soon Jay. That it was easier to fall into bed and forget about reality than to think about the future and what it might mean for them.

Especially when she could sense there was still a distance between them.

It was hard to put her finger on, but she could feel it. There was a part of him that wasn't fully committed to this reunion. Perhaps she could more easily pick up on it because she was doing the same thing. She was scared to take his words at face value, trust him with her heart and get crushed again. Maybe both of them were too nervous to think this second chance was truly a second chance.

Then again, those weren't the words of a man just looking for a distraction or a mother for the child he'd inherited. He meant it when he said he would make time for her. That he was proud of her. So maybe she was imagining things. Or perhaps the distance was natural after everything they'd been through and the gap between them would close in time. If they put in the effort.

"I would like you to come. It's black tie. April really went all out for this one. I'm so nervous I'm going to screw this opportunity up."

"I don't know why you'd be nervous, Scarlet. You're an amazing artist. San Francisco is lucky to have one of your galleries and all those people coming to the opening know it. Everyone is going to want a Scarlet Spencer original hanging above their mantel." Mason stopped and, with a frown, turned to their own bedroom fireplace. "You know, *we* don't even have a Scarlet Spencer hanging above *our* mantel. We just have some dumb old flat-screen television."

Scarlet smiled. "Thank you for agreeing to come with me." She leaned into him, snaking her arms around his waist and resting her head against his chest. "I'll see what I can do about the fireplace art," she added with a chuckle.

"You do that," he said with a low laugh that rumbled against her cheek. "And while you do that…" Mason began just as she felt her bath towel slip to the floor. "Oops." He grinned.

Scarlet didn't resist. Instead, she pressed her damp skin against him, letting her hard, chilled nipples dig into his shirt. She hadn't thought about having some alone time with Mason while they were on the trip, but the idea certainly intrigued her now. A nice hotel room. No baby. No nanny. No household to deal with. It sounded perfect.

Her worries about her opening faded as Mason tipped her backward over his arm and brought her uptilted breast to his mouth. He drew hard on the dark pink flesh, nipping just enough with his teeth to make her gasp and suck a ragged breath into her lungs.

"Shh…" Mason whispered as he brought a finger to his lips and then dragged it lazily between her breasts. "We don't want to wake Luna. But this weekend, you can make all the noise you want. No one will be around to hear you scream my name until you're hoarse."

"And what exactly do you have in store for me that will make me scream like that?"

Mason stood her up and flashed and evil grin. "You'll just have to wait and see."

Nine

This was Scarlet's biggest and fanciest gallery opening yet. They had a prime location at Fisherman's Wharf near one of her murals. It would draw in plenty of tourist foot traffic along with fans who were deliberately coming to the gallery itself, and she'd need every one to support the rent in such a pricey area of town. She felt like she should've been focused on every detail of the event, from which painting hung where to what hors d'oeuvres were being passed by the waiters, but she found her mind was elsewhere tonight.

She knew April could handle it. That was what she paid her for. She was the management, Scarlet was the talent.

"Did we leave Carroll with the pediatrician's phone number in case Luna gets sick again? She was still a little sniffly when we left."

Mason came up behind her as she stood in front of the mirror, putting on her earrings. His black Armani tuxedo fit him like a glove, highlighting his broad shoulders and narrow waist from years paddling out on his surfboard. It had been a long time since she'd seen him dressed up like this. He wore suits almost every day, but he only pulled this tux out for special occasions. Like their wedding day.

That felt like an eternity ago, and yet he hadn't changed a bit. Well, maybe there was a stray strand of gray at his temple and a few lines around his eyes, but he was still the man she said yes to all those years ago.

He smiled and patted at her bare shoulder. "Yes. She has all the numbers, I promise. The house is filled with enough food and baby supplies to last through a nuclear winter. It's just a two-day trip. Carroll knows what she's doing. Everything will be fine."

Scarlet fastened her earring and turned around to face him with a wry smile twisting her lips. "I'm being *that mom*, aren't I?"

He just smiled. "A good mom, yes. Good moms worry. But tonight, I want you to focus on you. It's your big opening. Everyone is coming out to see your work. I want you to focus on that and only that." He leaned in and pressed a soft kiss to the tip of her nose so her lipstick didn't smear. "Are you almost ready? The car is waiting downstairs."

Scarlet nodded and took a deep breath before grabbing her beaded navy clutch. "How do I look?" she asked, before turning to face him.

The look on Mason's face said it all. His blue gaze took in every inch of her body, from the navy-and-silver lace cap sleeves to the fitted, beaded bodice and full, draped skirt. She thought the color would look nice against her skin and complement the ocean colors of the paintings in her gallery. He seemed to agree. By the time his eyes met hers again, there was a huge, devious smile crossing his face. Even his dimples were showing.

"I think we should skip it," Mason said. He pressed up against her and rested his hands at her waist. "I think you need to take that dress off right now so I can start all those wicked things I promised to do to you."

Scarlet smacked him on the chest with her bag. "Well, I'm glad you approve of the dress, but that isn't happening. I can't be hoarse when I greet all my guests. But after we get back…" She trailed off with a seductive smile as she twisted out of his grasp. "Let's go."

Reluctantly, Mason followed her out of their suite and down to the lobby. Under the portico of the hotel, as predicted, a black town car with the name "Spencer" in the window was waiting for them.

It didn't take long to get to the gallery. They'd chosen a hotel only a few blocks from Fisherman's Wharf. They pulled up to the back entrance, where they could slip inside and check on things before the guests arrived.

"We're opening the doors in five," April barked into her headset as she blew past them in a black beaded cocktail dress. She stopped short in front of them. "Good, the guest of honor is in the building." She smiled, paying particular attention to Mason in his tuxedo. "You both look lovely tonight."

Scarlet caught a hint of a blush on his cheeks. "Thanks. Are we ready to go?"

April looked down at her watch. "Yep, let's get this party started."

From there, the first two hours were a blur. Mason stayed at her side for support but allowed himself to blend into the background while Scarlet took center stage. As she moved across the dance floor to greet guests and speak with people about her work, she would look over her shoulder and catch glimpses of him beaming with pride over his half-empty flute of champagne.

It was going well. At least she thought so. One of her massive original oils had been purchased for a solid six figures before Scarlet had finished her first drink. Smaller pieces were flying off the walls, figuratively, even with five-digit price tags. Almost everyone was leaving with at least an autographed coffee-table book or print. It was a great start to the gallery, which would need the capital to recoup the expense of opening up a new location.

It wasn't until she finally sat down at a table to rest her feet that she was able to consider the event a success and relax. She had been too busy to worry about Luna or Mason or anything else aside from keeping a smile on her face, but the event was winding down at last.

She took a sip of her wine and turned to look for Mason. He'd slipped away for a moment while she was talking to the mayor, but he hadn't returned yet. That was when she spotted him on the far side of the room. His back was to her as he admired a painting on the wall. When he turned around and his gaze met hers, she felt a sizzle run across her skin. She missed the heat of his body at her side, the gentle press of his palm against her lower back. The expression on his face promised all that and more when the opening was over.

He finally strolled back across the gallery and stopped just in front of her. "Come with me," Mason said as he held out his hand.

The look he gave her made her knees like butter and she wasn't sure she could follow him onto the dance floor even if she wanted to. Knowing there were quite a few guests watching, however, she smiled and forced herself to follow him.

A few couples were dancing around the center of the gallery. When the gala was over, one of her bronze sculptures would go in the open space, but for tonight, there was enough room for a dozen couples to dance to the soft jazz the band was playing.

They found an open spot and Mason wrapped his arm around her waist and held her tight against him. Scarlet adjusted in his arms and let him guide her in a soft rocking motion. Neither of them were very accomplished when it came to dancing, but they made do at events like this. It helped that she was always so aware of Mason's body. Every inch of him pressed into her, so she noted every twitch of muscle, every motion to guide her one way or another. She could almost anticipate his moves.

For the first time since they touched down in San Francisco, Scarlet felt like she had a moment to breathe. Even though April handled most everything, Scarlet still felt as though she had to double-check it all, practically rearranging artwork as Mason shoved her out the door so they could return to the hotel and change. Once the guests arrived, it was chatting and smiling and autographing books. She wasn't an introvert at heart, but there was no denying this was exhausting.

She was happy to just be in Mason's arms now. A month ago, it was a place she never thought she'd be again. On lonely nights, she'd lain in bed trying to remember the last time he'd kissed her, or the last time they'd made love. She couldn't even begin to recall when they'd danced. Maybe on the cruise they took to Mexico for their fifth anniversary.

"I can't remember the last time we had a night like this," he said in a low voice after a few quiet moments of dancing together. It was as though he could read her thoughts sometimes.

"Like what?" she asked, curious of how he'd come up with it.

"Just the two of us together. Dancing, drinking adult beverages and chatting about idle pursuits. There's no talk of babies or ovulation, family law attorneys or sperm counts. It's just you and me, enjoying a night together for the first time in forever. The last few years of our marriage were taken over by our quest to have a child. It's nice to just be Mason and Scarlet Spencer, married couple out for a night together, for a change."

Scarlet felt a rush of blood flood her cheeks in embarrassment. That probably wasn't the reaction he was expecting, but she couldn't help it. She knew that most of that life disruption was her doing. She was the one who got obsessed and dragged him along with her. "I'm sorry I let all that get in the way of us. I just went baby crazy and forgot all about our marriage."

"You didn't forget about our marriage," he soothed. "You just got focused on our family. There are worse things."

"Yes, but we lost each other along the way."

"We didn't lose each other. We just forgot we were supposed to face those trials as a team. Somehow we turned into adversaries instead."

It had felt that way for a while, even though she knew, practically, that it wasn't true. There was no bad guy to blame their fertility difficulties on, no villain to accuse of stealing Evan away. It was just life making a turn in a direction that neither of them knew how to handle. They'd accomplished everything they'd set out to do in life, but this one thing had just been out of their reach.

"Are we playing on the same team now?" she asked. "For good?" It was a question she'd been afraid to pose since Mason moved back into the house. When the temporary started to feel permanent, how was she to know what was real anymore?

"We are, Scarlet. I told you I wasn't going to run away again. I meant it. I've been happier with you these last few weeks than I've been in a long time. I'm not letting that slip away again."

He looked down at her with his big blue eyes and she felt the last of her fears slip away. This was really happening. They were reconciling, and not just because of the baby, but because they wanted to be together. They realized they were better together. Luna was just the fluffy pink icing on the cake.

"I'm happy to hear you say that," Scarlet said.

Mason smiled. "And I'll be happy to sweep you

off your feet and back to our hotel suite. How long do we have to stay?"

Scarlet eyed the dwindling crowd and April in the corner rubbing her feet. Once her manager's shoes came off, it was safe to call it a night.

"Not a minute longer."

Mason was glad to be back at their hotel. As he tugged at his bow tie and pulled it out from under his collar, he could only shake his head. "Are they always like that?" he asked.

Scarlet's reflection in the mirror smiled at him as she stepped out of her shoes and pulled off her jewelry. "That one was fancier than normal, but yes, they're all basically the same. I suck up to people, they buy my art." She walked up to him and then turned her back toward him. "Can you unzip me, please?"

"With pleasure." Mason reached for her zipper at her neck. Tonight, she'd worn her long dark hair twisted up into an elegant sort of knot. The whole back of the gown was navy lace, giving glimpses of her bare back down all the way to the swell of her hips. Grasping the zipper tab, he slowly followed the curve of her spine until it settled at the bottom.

Before she could pull away, he pushed the lace aside with his hands and exposed her back. The cap sleeves moved easily down her arms until the dress was pooled around her waist. The mirror she'd stood at moments before now gave him the perfect view of his wife's full, bare breasts. He watched their reflection as he snaked his arms beneath hers and cupped her breasts in his hands.

Scarlet sighed and leaned back against him. He loved the feeling of her body pressed into his own. He loved the warmth of her skin, the scent of her hair, the soft sounds she made as he teased and pinched her nipples into tight buds... He watched her face contort with pleasure as he caressed her the way he knew she liked to be touched. She was his wife. His everything. They'd been together for almost his entire adult life. He knew that a kiss just below her earlobe would make her crazy with need. He knew that she was ticklish behind her knees. He didn't need a road map for her body because he already knew it by heart. Returning to the familiar territory had been both comforting and exciting after the months apart.

Now that she was back in his arms, in his bed and in his heart for good, the thought sent a surge of desire and possessiveness through his veins. She was his now, and no paperwork from their lawyers was going to change that.

Scarlet tipped her head enough to reach up and pluck a few pins from her hair. It was enough for the entire twist to come tumbling down over her shoulders. The scent of her skin mingled with her styling products to surround him with a smell that, when his eyes were closed, instantly brought to mind images of her in their bathroom. He leaned in and buried his face in her hair, letting the silky strands brush over his skin before drawing a deep breath of her into his lungs.

She arched her back and shimmied her hips

just enough for the gown to fall to her feet. That left the ample curves of her thong-clad rear end to press into the desire that strained against his tuxedo pants. He growled low in her ear as the sensation radiated through his lower extremities.

"Do you know how badly I wanted to rip that gown off you tonight?" he whispered. "I wanted to make love to you on the floor of the stock room and I didn't care if April caught us in the act. That's why I had to walk away for a while. I couldn't take it."

"Well, it's out of your way now," she said. She stepped out of her dress and moved away from him, leaving him suddenly cold and alone. When she turned to face him at the foot of the bed, she was wearing nothing but a nude lace thong that blended into her skin and nearly vanished.

He couldn't tear his eyes away as he slipped out of his tuxedo jacket and unbuttoned his shirt. "Good. I'd hate to ruin a perfectly nice dress."

Still in his tuxedo pants, Mason closed the gap she'd created between them and placed his hands on the soft curve of her hips. He tugged her against him, pressing his need into her stomach. "Do you have any idea what you do to me? What you've always done to me?"

Scarlet wrapped her arms around his neck and laced her fingers through the short strands of his hair. "I've got a pretty good idea." She looked up at him with her big doe eyes and batted her lashes coquettishly. "But maybe you should show me just to make sure."

She knew just how to play to his base instincts. With a growl, he scooped her up off the ground. She squealed and clung to him, wrapping her legs around his waist as he carried her over to the bed. The sound of her carefree laughter was like music to his ears after all the seriousness they'd faced lately. He was glad that this time, he was the one making her smile.

Once he reached the bed, he laid her down with her legs still entwined around his waist. He surged forward, pinning her against the mattress and pressing his length against her lace-covered center. She moaned at the contact, but his mouth quickly sought out hers and swallowed the sound. He drank in the taste of her, relishing in the mix of dry white wine and sweet chocolate truffles that still lingered on her tongue from the party.

She squirmed beneath him, and the next thing he knew, he could feel her palm pressed against the fly of his trousers. He shuddered and ripped his mouth away from hers. "Quit that," he groaned.

Instead, she slipped her hand beneath his waistband and wrapped her fingers around his length. He swore against the pillows before propping on his elbow and tugging her hand away. He sat back on his knees, and gripping both her wrists together in one hand, he pinned them against the mattress over her head. She tried to break free from his grasp, but she wasn't getting away.

"You're naughty, and this is your punishment."

Scarlet looked at him with wide, innocent eyes, then lifted her hips to drag the crotch of her panties against him. Apparently, she didn't need hands to torture him.

"Do you want to be in charge tonight?" he asked.

She answered him with a grin. Fair enough. He released her arms and rolled to the right, taking her with him until he was lying on his back and she was straddling him.

"I'm all yours," Mason said.

"You always have been," Scarlet replied.

Mason pressed his fingertips into the flesh of her hips and looked up at her with a serious expression in a previously light moment. "I always will be."

Scarlet stilled over him. Her eyes grew glassy for a moment before she smiled through her tears. She didn't respond. Instead, she sat back on her heels and lifted her hair up with her arms, putting on a little show for him. He wanted to reach for her and tug her close, but he was letting her have tonight. It was her big night, anyway.

She stretched, arching her back and letting her

silky chestnut waves rain back down onto her shoulders. She rocked her hips with the movement, torturing him further through the cursed pants he'd made the mistake of leaving on. As if she could anticipate his discomfort, Scarlet climbed onto her knees and reached down to unfasten his pants. She slid them and his silk boxers down his legs, then let him kick them off onto the floor.

Reaching between them, she wrapped her fingers around him, and this time he didn't complain. Mason closed his eyes and exhaled hard through his nose as sparks of pleasure danced across his skin. She stroked the length of him once, twice, and then he felt her velvet heat envelop him.

He opened his eyes to find Scarlet straddling him with a look of divine contentment on her face. She started rocking slowly, making him clench his teeth. He wasn't sure how long he could stand her moving like this. "Come here, baby," he managed through his tightly flexed jaw.

Thankfully, Scarlet opted not to torture him any longer. She leaned forward, planting her elbows on the mattress beside his head. Now she was close enough for him to lean up and capture her lips. As their tongues and breath mingled together, she continued to rock back and forth. Wrapping his arms tight around her waist, he stilled her movement and began thrusting into her from beneath.

Her sobbing gasps against his mouth were enough to tell him that she didn't mind his interference. He could feel her body stiffen against him as she came closer to her release. He waited with anticipation for the moment to come. Maybe even more so than for his own orgasm. Watching the beautiful woman he called his own come apart in his arms was something he could never tire of. He longed for it, needed it for his own satisfaction to be complete.

"Yes," he whispered against the line of her jaw, following his words with soft kisses. He gripped her hips harder, thrusting into her with renewed enthusiasm. "Please, baby. I need to hear it. Be as loud as you need to be tonight."

Scarlet closed her eyes then, her mouth open in anticipation of the tsunami coming for her. When it hit, he held her tight, riding the wave with her as she cried out into the room. "Mason!" She pushed herself up, gripping his shoulders and bucking her hips against him.

Mason felt her muscles tighten and flutter around him, pushing him toward his own end. When she collapsed against his chest, he wrapped his arms around her. The feel of her skin on his, her breath at his ear, her moist core wrapped around him…it took only a few more thrusts before he lost himself inside her.

For a few minutes, all Mason could hear was the sound of their breathing and the rapid pounding of his heart in his chest. It was the first time in a long time that the beat of his heart tapped out a joyful rhythm instead of a somber dirge. With Scarlet still in his arms, he felt happy. Really, truly happy.

Reluctantly, he let her finally roll back onto the bed. They crawled beneath the blankets together and switched off the lamp before he turned on his side and pulled her back against him. It had been a great night. He almost didn't want to close his eyes and have it end, but sleep was winning the fight tonight.

Mason was very nearly on the edge of sleep when he heard his cell phone ringing on the nightstand. Rolling over in bed, he picked up his phone and his heart sank when he saw the number. The fleeting moments of happiness he'd just cherished seemed to crumble in his hands as he looked at the screen. The last time he got a late-night call like this, it was Jay telling him that Rachel had an accident and was dead. This time, with the hospice number flashing across the screen, there was only one eventuality and he wasn't prepared for it.

Ignoring the call wouldn't change anything, however. He hit the button to answer. "Hello?"

"Hello, this is Karen with New Horizons Rehabilitation Center. Is this Mr. Spencer speaking?"

He closed his eyes and hesitated to answer, knowing his life was about to change forever. "This is he."

Ten

It felt surreal to be back to the cemetery so soon. They all knew this was where they were going to return, but that just wasn't something Scarlet had been ready to face.

Today, they were seated in a short row of chairs in front of the casket. That made it easier to hold the squirming Luna in her arms. For some reason, holding the baby made her feel grounded. It couldn't hide the ugly reality of the situation from her, though. As her gaze strayed from Jay's casket, she noticed the grass hadn't even started to grow over Rachel's grave. They'd removed the last of the dead flowers from her service to prepare Jay's final resting place.

A new wreath of white roses was placed behind the newly installed headstone Rachel shared with her husband. All his information was complete aside from the date of his death, a date that Scarlet would never forget. Up until the moment they received that call, it had been one of the best days of her life. Since then, everything had fallen apart.

They'd called the airline after getting off the phone and made arrangements to catch the first flight back to LAX. They didn't even bother going back to sleep. Instead, they'd taken showers, packed and checked out of the hotel in the small hours of the morning.

Mason had said almost nothing since he got the call. He'd hung up the phone and said, "Jay's dead. I'm sorry, but we need to get back to LA." That was basically it. He'd muttered the occasional inconsequential thing about packing and spoken briefly to the TSA agents at the airport, but Scarlet was suddenly invisible.

At least that was how she felt. She wanted to hug him. To say she was sorry about Jay. But he wouldn't make eye contact long enough to engage her in any kind of serious conversation. After they got back home, things weren't much better. He immediately threw himself into dealing with Jay's funeral arrangements. He met with Jay's estate attorneys and busied himself with paperwork for Luna's adoption.

Scarlet tried not to notice that he never once mentioned her adopting Luna. She wasn't sure if that indicated a change in how he felt about their relationship or not. What she did know was that it felt like before. Like the months leading up to their separation. The warm, affectionate Mason seemed to have vanished with that phone call. He hadn't touched her. Some nights, he hadn't even come upstairs to go to bed.

This morning, like the night before, she'd woken up to a cold, pristine space beside her in the bed. It was amazing how quickly she'd gotten used to having him back there. It was where he belonged. Scarlet just wasn't sure if he felt the same way any longer.

She'd held her tongue so far. She understood that Mason would need time and space to grieve. His younger brother had been his best friend. That didn't mean she wasn't worried. If Mason retreated too far into himself, if he didn't lean on Scarlet for support the way a husband should lean on his wife…she worried that he was going to run.

Mason had sworn he wouldn't run again. He said that he wanted her, that he wanted this. But Jay's death was their first real test, and a serious one at that. If his instinct was to flee from the reality of losing his brother, he might be several miles down the road before he realized that he was doing it again.

It felt like running. As she turned to look at Mason, he was like a stone statue. No emotion, no movement. She hadn't seen him cry a single time since he got the call about his brother. He'd instantly gone into "handle it" mode. She wished he would cry. Then she could feel like comforting him wasn't a misplaced gesture. He was sitting a mere five inches away from Scarlet, but it felt like she was losing him all over again and she didn't know what to do.

Scarlet turned away from Mason and looked to the minister. The same man had overseen Rachel's service. She was certain his words were comforting, but she had a hard time focusing on him. She was trying to keep from letting her feelings get the best of her for Luna's sake. The baby might not understand what was happening, but she could feel the emotional energy Scarlet put out. She didn't want Luna wailing through the service. It would break everyone's hearts to hear the dead couple's baby so distraught.

"Let us give thanks today, even in our grief, for Jay's brother, Mason, and his wife, Scarlet."

Scarlet perked up at the sound of her name spoken by the minister.

"For even in this moment of sadness and mourning, we are celebrating the beginning of a new family for Luna when she needs one the most. For many years Mason and Scarlet have longed for a child, and now they have found what they always hoped for. The Lord works in mysterious ways, bringing joy to some even as grief is brought to another. But may we find peace in knowing it was God's plan for Rachel and Jay to be together in the Kingdom of Heaven, and for Luna to remain on Earth with her new family."

Scarlet looked out of the corner of her eye at Mason. He seemed to be even more uncomfortable than he had been before. He obviously didn't like the attention shifted onto them, as though they had somehow benefited from his brother's death. She was certain no one looked at it that way, but still, he seemed visibly uneasy.

She turned her attention to Luna instead. The baby was enamored with the stuffed monkey they brought with them today. It was one of the few items they could take that didn't jingle, beep, play music or otherwise disrupt the service. Luna chewed at the monkey's ear, indicating another tooth was coming in. A milestone her parents would miss.

And then, as soon as it had begun, the service was over. Mason and Jay's parents approached the casket to say goodbye, and then Scarlet stood and went with Mason. She watched as Mason laid his hand against the smooth white surface. He said something she couldn't understand, then turned and walked down the hill to the car. She followed behind him, struggling to catch up in her heels as he nearly ran from his brother's grave site.

By the time she reached the Range Rover, Mason was inside and the engine was running. Scarlet cautiously buckled Luna into her car seat and climbed in front. "For a moment I wasn't sure if you were leaving without us," she said quietly after she shut the door.

Mason didn't look at her. He just put the car

into Drive and pulled away from the curb. "Don't be ridiculous," he replied.

"It felt like you were running."

"I…" He hesitated. "I just needed to get away from there. It was too much all at once."

Scarlet turned to look at him. "Not from the service. It felt like you were running away from me."

He considered her words for a moment before pulling out into traffic and taking the turn to merge onto the freeway. "Maybe I was," he admitted with a heavy sigh.

Scarlet didn't know what to say to that. She had expected him to argue with her. To tell her she was being too sensitive and this wasn't about her. To reassure her that he wasn't running away, he'd promised he wouldn't do that, and that he just needed some time. She'd gotten the exact opposite and it stunned her into silence.

The ache of worry started to pool in her stomach. Had she misjudged this entire situation?

She sat back against the soft leather of the passenger seat and took a deep breath. Mason had only asked her to play along with the relationship for Jay's sake. Once his brother passed, the charade was supposed to end. She knew that. But hadn't things changed between them? Hadn't they made love, made promises that they weren't going to let their marriage fall apart when things got hard? She hadn't imagined that things had evolved past the original agreement, had she?

And yet she knew that was Mason's modus operandi. When he couldn't control things, he retreated. And now, despite everything he may have said before, everything he promised to change, he was distancing himself from her and their marriage. She could feel it: the same anxious ache of losing something and being unable to stop it that she'd felt before he left the last time.

Tigers didn't change their stripes.

Scarlet could feel things spiraling out of her control. She hadn't wanted the divorce last time and it hadn't made any difference. Once he pulled away, there was nothing left to hold on to. She wanted to work through this, to raise Luna with him the way Jay had always intended. She just wasn't certain if Mason was going to give her that choice.

Luna.

Scarlet closed her eyes tight and clutched at the leather armrest as she realized how much more was at stake if he ran away this time. He wouldn't. He couldn't. After weeks of insisting he wanted them to be a family, he wouldn't take the baby away just when she'd given in and fallen in love with her. Or would he? If the situation was uncomfortable enough for him, she wasn't so certain.

"And were you running from Luna, too?" she asked.

Mason exited the freeway and pulled to a stop at a red light. His jaw tightened as he gripped the steering wheel and considered his words. "Of course not. I told my brother that I would raise Luna like she was my own daughter and I intend to keep my promise."

"And what about all the promises you made to me?" she asked.

He didn't answer.

Mason felt like crap. There was no candy coating it.

He was used to things going to plan. In his business, he was in charge of every detail and had built his success on knowing the right decisions to make and executing them flawlessly. Real life wasn't as simple as choosing which brand and style of beach towels to stock in the stores. There was an X factor of emotion that threw everything into a tailspin no matter how hard he tried to keep things steady.

As he sat at the dining room table, staring at his laptop and surrounded by paperwork, he could feel that X factor at play. Nothing was going the way he expected it to. Or at least the way he wanted it to. That just added a foul mood on top of his other problems. He missed his brother, missed his wife, missed feeling like his life made any sense at all…

He'd seen the way Scarlet looked at him since the funeral. He'd earned that scowl, there was no question of it. But for now, he needed his space. He needed room to breathe, to think. Being with Scarlet made him happy. This was not the appropriate time to be happy.

It was like some kind of self-imposed penance that he was sure Scarlet wouldn't understand. All he knew was that the moment before he'd received the call about Jay's passing, he'd been happier than he'd been in years. He had his wife back, his home back, a child he adored, things were going well… It was almost enough to make a man forget that his sister-in-law was newly buried and his brother was clinging to life in a hospice facility. That the baby they cherished—the one who had salvaged their marriage and made their lives complete—had only arrived through the direst of circumstances. Rachel and Jay had to lose everything, including their lives, for Mason and Scarlet to be happy again.

Mason felt guilty as hell. That was the long and short of it. His life was better than ever and he'd forgotten in the moment that he had no business celebrating at a time like this. The only way he knew to make up for it was to make his brother's needs his number one priority. The funeral arrangements were an easy and obvious way to fill his time. From there, he spent hours with the estate lawyers determining what needed to be done with Jay and Rachel's property and holdings. It would all be liquidated and put into a trust for Luna. Jay had already put that provision in his will.

In preparing for Luna's adoption, his brother had also put together an account for her care. It was generous enough that the monthly interest generated on the principal would handle most of her expenses. Not that a one-year-old had many outside of the usual food, diapers and care. Later, however, it would provide for private school and the best colleges she could get into.

Mason would've happily paid for all of that himself. He told Jay he would raise Luna as his own daughter and that meant he wouldn't skimp when it came to anything she might need. At this point, he'd feel better about things if he was financially supporting Luna. But Jay hadn't allowed for it. It was typical Jay to handle all the details so Mason didn't have to do anything but make the most of his time with Luna.

But that was the hardest part of all. At least for Mason.

Luna wouldn't remember her parents, or know why she was here instead of the home she'd been born in. But Mason knew, and every time he looked at her, all he could see was everything she'd lost. Each milestone she achieved would be bittersweet, knowing Rachel and Jay had missed it.

"There you are."

Mason looked up to find Scarlet peeking at

him from around the corner. He had set up his computer in the dining room, which was in plain view, but was also the most secluded and unused of the rooms in the house. "Hey."

Scarlet leaned against the wall and crossed her arms over her chest. "Do you know that's the first thing you've said to me all day?"

He frowned. It wasn't intentional. At least he didn't think so. "I've been working on some things today."

She nodded thoughtfully. "Just like yesterday. And the day before. And every day since Jay died."

Mason sat back in his chair and slammed his laptop lid shut. "Someone has to deal with things, Scarlet. My parents can't handle it."

"I know. And I understand. But you don't have to abandon your own family to do it, Mason."

"I don't know what you're talking about, Scarlet. I'm right here. I haven't gone anywhere."

"Physically, no. Mentally, you've checked out of this marriage. And of this family, too."

Mason pushed his chair back and stood up. He grabbed his drink off the table and carried it into the kitchen for a refill. He needed something to do instead of sit there while she leveled accusations at him. "Don't you think you're being a little overdramatic about all of this? My brother died. Can't I have a little time to process everything?"

Scarlet followed him into the kitchen. "Absolutely. And if I thought you were actually working through your brother's death, I wouldn't mind at all. But you're hiding from it just as surely as you're hiding from us. I know this feeling, Mason. You're getting ready to run."

Mason set his glass on the counter and turned to face her. "Do I look like someone about to run away?" He was wearing cargo shorts and flip-flops.

"I didn't think so. I thought you really meant it when you said you wanted to try again."

"I did want to try again. But then I saw this and I wasn't sure you felt the same way." Mason

"Scarlet, please," he said, his voice on the edge of begging. "Can we not do this today?"

"When, then, Mason? You're not exactly known for facing issues head-on. Are you going to drag it out for months this time and then walk away when I'm least expecting it?"

"What does it hurt to wait instead of acting in haste or on an emotional response? I'm dealing with a lot right now. I don't understand why you can't give me the space I need so we can have this discussion when we're better prepared."

"Because...every moment I spend with you and Luna is just another memory that's going to haunt me once you're gone."

That snapped Mason to attention. He looked up at her, the words surprising him. "What?"

Scarlet just shook her head and let her gaze fall to the floor. His brilliant artist, his loving wife, looked completely broken. Her tall, strong frame seemed to be swallowed by her sweatshirt, and her messy ponytail seemed more the result of stress than its usual casual ease. There were gray smudges beneath her dark eyes that he hadn't noticed before. The last few days had obviously been harder on her than he'd allowed himself to notice. He'd been too wrapped up in himself.

"I think I'm done, Mason."

"What do you mean by 'done'? Do you mean done with us?"

"Yes, I'm done. I can't handle any more of this emotional roller coaster. I can't be with you. I can't be in a relationship with someone that I can't depend on. You wanted this second chance, but I feel like you're just throwing it away, and me with it. Your brother is dead. I'm sorry. But you're not. I feel like you're punishing yourself for that, and punishing all of us in the process. I can't just sit around and wait for you to decide you don't want to do this anymore."

Mason watched Scarlet reach for the paperwork on the counter. She flipped through it, searching for the final page. She hesitated only for a moment before she reached for a pen and signed her name on the line. Mason held his breath in his throat as he watched her go through the motions of ending their marriage. She'd always fought to stay together before, but he could tell she was tired of fighting.

"There," she said, looking up at him with a shimmer of tears in her dark eyes. "If you're really truly done, if you want to leave for whatever reason, I'm not going to be the one who keeps you here against your will. If you want to go, sign the papers and send them to your attorney. If you don't, tear them up and snap out of this haze you're in. But I'm tired of being in limbo with you, so you have to choose."

Setting down the pen with an angry slap against the granite, Scarlet avoided eye contact with him and walked out of the kitchen.

Mason stood stunned for a moment. He wasn't entirely sure what to do. Things had escalated between them faster than he'd anticipated. Apparently, his internal struggle had pushed Scarlet to the edge. Walking up to the counter, he picked up the papers and looked at her angrily scribbled signature on the last page.

Her name in ink on their divorce papers was a jarring sight. Maybe this whole exercise for Jay's sake had just been putting off the inevitable. For a while he'd thought that maybe they could have that happy family they'd talked about and dreamed of. Now he knew it was just a pipe dream.

He and Scarlet were done. They'd been done for months. They just hadn't wanted to admit it to themselves because the alternative was scary for them both. But it didn't change the truth.

Mason carried the papers over to the dining room table with everything else and slammed them onto the top of the pile. One more thing to deal with.

Eleven

Scarlet stayed at the office as late as possible. She didn't want to go home because she knew what she would find—an empty house and an empty heart. Mason hadn't said a word to her since their discussion, but he'd returned to sleeping in her studio that night. She saw him packing up a few things from the bathroom as she left this morning. That meant he would be gone by the time she got home. And if he was gone, that meant everything she loved would be gone, too.

She knew the minute she signed those papers

that she'd made the wrong choice. She had given him an out, letting him decide once and for all if he wanted to be with her or not. She was giving him the freedom to make that choice without guilt. But as she'd signed the papers, essentially giving up on him, she'd watched the expression on his face completely crumple.

Up until that moment, it was what she thought he wanted. Mason was the one who never talked about their future together in concrete terms. The moment he seemed to break down and say yes, he would commit to this marriage and this family, he seemed to take a huge step back from everything. After the funeral, he'd been more distant than he had been in the weeks leading up to his moving out the first time. It had become clear to Scarlet that he was pulling away now that Jay was gone. She'd assumed that in his mind the game they'd been playing was over.

When he pulled out those divorce papers, his response to them had thrown her completely off guard. Somehow, he was upset with her because he thought she'd been conniving behind his back to steal custody of Luna away. That was hardly the case. Did he really think she was capable of seducing him, luring him into her life, then just casting him aside once she was able to secure the baby she wanted? They'd been together too many years for him to accuse her of something like that.

Her heart had broken in that moment—what was left of it at least. There had only been fragments when he came back into her life and now there was nothing. She'd given what she had left to him and Luna.

When she walked into their home tonight—the home that had been so full of life and excitement the last few weeks—she knew it wouldn't be the same. It would be silent. Hollow. She'd experienced that before, although it would be so much worse this time because she wasn't just losing Mason, she was losing Luna, too. She'd given the sweet baby extra kisses this morning before hurrying out the door so Carroll couldn't see her tears.

A rush of movement passed Scarlet's office door, then the figure stopped and leaned back. It was April, with a perplexed look on her face. "What are you doing here? I thought you were taking some time away after the funeral."

Scarlet could only shrug. If she opened her mouth, she would start to cry. She hadn't told anyone about what had happened between her and Mason. She wasn't sure if she was ready to say those words out loud. She'd spent the hours focused on going over the San Francisco opening numbers and orders for the next month.

"I am," she managed to say.

April backed up and came into her office, sitting down in her guest chair. "What's going on? You're almost never in the office. Things at home must be rough. Is Mason taking his brother's death hard?"

"You could say that. He's also taking the divorce hard." Once the *D* word slipped from her lips, Scarlet felt a rush of emotion and heat warm her cheeks. Tears spilled down her face before she could squeeze her eyes closed.

"Divorce? Wait. What happened? Oh, honey," April continued, holding a tissue out to Scarlet.

Scarlet reached out to take it and press the thin paper to her face. It was hardly enough to hide behind, but it soaked up a few of her tears and made her feel a little better. She hated to fall apart in front of other people.

April gave her the space she needed, thankfully. She sat quietly for a few moments before she pressed Scarlet to talk again. "So tell me what's happened."

She crumpled the tissue into a ball in her fist and shook her head. "It's done."

"Was that his decision this time or yours?"

"I don't really know." Scarlet bit at her bottom lip. She knew how ridiculous that sounded, but it was true. She didn't want the divorce, but she wasn't going to sit around and wait for him to leave her either. Either they were staying together forever or she was going to end it while she still had some of her heart and pride left to salvage.

"He was pulling away like last time. I could see it happening no matter how hard I tried to engage him. So this time, I pushed him instead of trying to pull him back. I thought maybe that would snap him into fighting back. Fighting to be with me or at the very least standing up and saying, 'Relax, I'm not about to leave you every time I need some space.' But I think I pushed too hard and he thought I wanted him gone, because he just walked away. So I guess it's my fault. But I couldn't sit around and wait for him to leave me in good time. I would rather the break be clean and fast."

"Are you taking it better this time? Being clean and fast?" April asked.

"No." Scarlet broke down into tears again. She hated April seeing her cry, but she couldn't stop the emotion from pouring out of her even if she wanted to.

"If you don't want this, why don't you talk to

him? Tell him that you're just scared of losing him and you don't really want a divorce. It's not too late to change things."

"He's already moved out."

"He's moved out before and come back. That doesn't mean anything."

"The only reason he came back before was to make his brother happy. Whatever I may have thought the last few weeks were, or ended up being, it all started as a ruse. Maybe I was a fool for seeing more to it than there really was."

April got up and came around the desk. "Give me a hug," she insisted. Scarlet got up and let herself be embraced by her significantly smaller manager. It reminded her of the hugs from her grandmother who had been just shy of five feet tall. She gave the best hugs, though, making Scarlet feel safe and loved even when she had far outgrown her lap.

"You need to go home," April said as they finally parted.

Scarlet shook her head adamantly. "I can't. I

can't bear to see the house empty again. I had everything I ever wanted in my hands and I let it slip away because I was too frightened to hold on tight enough."

"You can't sleep here. You can stay here for a week and it won't change what's at home. Face your fears. Go home. Think about what has happened and see if you're inspired to do the brave, hard thing."

"And what's that?"

"Going to someone with your heart on your sleeve and saying you were wrong. That you were scared. There's no way to judge how Mason will take it, but it's possible that he feels the same way but you two don't know how to talk to one another. Share your feelings."

"And what if he doesn't feel the same way?"

"Then you'll have me over for drinks, we'll have a good cry and you'll move on knowing you did everything that you could."

She was right. Scarlet knew she was right. With

a sigh, she reached for her purse and shut down her computer. "Okay. Thank you."

"Call me if you need me," April said as Scarlet slipped out the door.

Her manager's pep talk got her into her car, but it didn't help for the long drive home through LA traffic. With every mile the anticipation built. Anticipation for what she would find at home. For how Mason would take her confession. She knew that all of that was out of her control. April was right about doing what was in her power, telling him how she felt and letting the cards fall where they may.

When the garage door opened, it revealed, as expected, that both Mason's and Carroll's cars were gone. There was a part of her, up until that moment, that thought she was wrong about what she would find there. That maybe Mason might've decided to fight for her love instead of walking away again. That instead of doing what he thought was best, he would tear up the divorce papers and say, "No, I'm not letting us throw our relationship away again, no matter what it costs us."

Those were just the kind of heroics that happened only in movies and romantic novels. In real life, the garage was empty, the house was empty and so was the cavernous hole in her aching chest.

She opened the door, cautiously peeking into the quiet, dark kitchen. The house was perfectly still, reminding her of those days before Mason returned. With a sigh, she came inside and shut the door behind her. The silence was familiar, at least, as was the heartache. She knew how to handle that.

There was a new element to this emptiness, however, that she wasn't so sure about. Setting her purse on the kitchen counter, she looked around. There were no glass bottles in the dish rack with Mason's travel mug. No brightly colored plastic spoons mixed in with the other handwashed utensils. She continued into the living room. His laptop wasn't on the coffee table and there was no Pack 'n Play by the couch.

Her heart was pounding in her ears as she turned toward the nursery door. It was as though it was once again the closed shrine she never entered. The monument to her lost child. She knew she couldn't let it become that way, no matter what was on the other side of the door.

She turned the knob and let the door swing open. There was nothing. Mason had taken the furniture, the toys, the clothes...nothing remained in the room but the mural she'd painted for Luna. She wished he could've taken that, too. Now, when she looked at it, all she could see was Luna's toothy grin as she squealed and tried to say *dolphin*.

That was the moment. The moment everything changed. Scarlet knew, she just knew how all this would end. That was why she'd insisted on the nanny and the hands-off approach for both Luna and Mason. She knew her heart would get captured by the tiny child and the bumbling uncle

who was in over his head. And she'd done it anyway. She'd let herself fall back in love with her
husband, let herself get attached to a child who
wasn't hers, and it all fell apart.

Standing in the middle of the room, Scarlet
looked up at the mural and felt her knees give out
from under her. She sank to the plush gray car-
pet and, now that she was well and truly alone,
let her grief unravel.

Mason looked out the massive window of his
Hollywood Hills home at the valley below and
missed the ocean more than ever. It had been
nearly two weeks since he'd moved out, but it
hadn't taken him five minutes to know he'd made
a huge mistake. He'd known that immediately,
felt it in his bones when he walked through the
front door.

He wasn't the only one. Luna didn't like it either. She didn't say as much, of course, but she'd
been miserably fussy lately. Carroll did her best
to soothe her, but there was nothing that warm

milk or her favorite toy could do. She wanted Scarlet.

And so did he.

There just wasn't anything he thought he could do about it now. He'd promised not to run away from her, and the moment things got tough, that's what he'd done. He hadn't realized it at the time. As always, he'd found a way to justify what he was doing. Someone needed to handle things. And that was true. But there wasn't so much to be done that he needed to withdraw from his wife and family.

He'd felt guilty, scared, unsure of the future, and he screwed up. Yes, Scarlet's signing the divorce papers had hurt, but in retrospect, he realized what she was doing. She'd pushed him to see which way he would turn under stress, and he did just what she was afraid of. He bolted back to Hollywood even though it was the last thing he really wanted to do.

Mason frowned at the layer of smog blanketing the valley and shifted his gaze to the courtyard below. Carroll and Luna were playing outside. He'd already called about having a swing set put in. In the meantime, Luna was happy with the small plastic playhouse with a window and a tiny slide.

Carroll helped her down the slide and Luna broke into a wide grin as she reached the bottom. It was the first time she'd smiled since they moved here. Maybe she was starting to forget Scarlet. She was so young. It would be a tragedy, though.

The last thing he wanted to do, especially after all their prior heartbreak, was to take a child away from Scarlet. Even when faced with the knowledge that she might be planning to take Luna from him, he would've said he couldn't do it to her. He'd seen how devastated she was losing Evan. Although he'd blamed himself for their inability to have a child, Scarlet insisted it wasn't his fault.

But losing Luna was his fault. He had taken her away. And just because he had every right to do it didn't make it okay. It wasn't what Rachel and Jay wanted. It wasn't what Scarlet wanted. And it certainly wasn't what he wanted. He just wasn't certain if what he wanted was what he should have.

Climb down from the cross, Mason. We don't need another martyr in this family.

The night before, Mason had shot up in bed in a cold sweat. He'd heard those words, his brother's words, as surely as if Jay had been sitting on the bed speaking to him. For a moment, Mason expected to actually see Jay sitting in the chair. Then he remembered his brother was dead and gone.

Perhaps it was his conscience telling him what Jay would say if he were alive. Out of the two brothers, Mason was driven by success and Jay was driven by happiness. Oddly enough, they were both successful in their own ways, but Jay's focus on being content had served him well. Mason felt guilty for being happy after his brother's life had imploded, but he failed to realize that Jay wouldn't see it that way at all. Jay would want his older brother to be happy, especially if that happiness resulted in a better life for Luna.

Jay would've reached out from his hospital bed and smacked Mason across the back of the head if he'd thought for one moment that Mason would sacrifice his own happiness out of guilt over Jay's and Rachel's deaths. He would be furious that Mason wasn't living his life to the fullest when he was lucky enough to still have one to live.

Of course, that just made Mason feel even guiltier. He couldn't win.

But if he was damned if he did, and damned if he didn't, he might as well choose to be guilty *and* happy, right? Jay would say yes. Scarlet would say yes. Why couldn't he let himself say yes, too?

He wanted to. He wanted to hold his wife again. The guilt would pass, but he needed to work through it. He wanted to see Luna fall asleep in Scarlet's arms. He'd promised Jay that he would give Luna the best possible upbringing. Didn't that mean having a mother who would love and care for her more than anything else?

And if he did choose to be happy, if he did want Scarlet back in their lives, was it a decision come too late?

Mason turned his back to the window and walked over to his desk. It was overrun with paperwork now instead of the kitchen table at the beach house. On top was the divorce paperwork with Scarlet's signature still on it. Mason hadn't signed. She probably thought that he'd signed and filed the paperwork the next day, but he hadn't. He couldn't make himself do it. That was admitting failure, and if there was one thing that made Mason more uncomfortable than guilt, it was defeat.

And if he refused to be defeated, he had to try to win Scarlet back. He sat on the edge of his bed trying to think about what he could do to woo his wife. The years had taught him that flowers, jewelry and the usual items were appreciated, but not particularly Scarlet's style. She was the kind that was impossible to shop for, the one who wanted something thoughtful and from the heart.

What could he possibly give her?

He would think of something and give it his best shot. If Scarlet wouldn't take him back, there was nothing he could do about it. He'd made his bed and now he had to lie in it. But he at least had to try. When he left before, he'd done it because he wanted her to have the family she really wanted, instead of believing that what she really wanted was him. He'd worried this time that Luna wouldn't be enough for her, but those doubts flew out the window the day he came home to the mural in progress.

Scarlet might not want to take him back, but that was a risk he'd have to take. He would march into the house with his heart on his sleeve and see what happened. Either way, he knew in his heart that he couldn't take Luna from her.

Wait…that was it.

Mason walked back over to his desk and started shuffling through the papers until he found the folder of adoption paperwork. He had been named Luna's physical and legal guardian prior to Jay's passing, but now they were starting the process of legal adoption.

Even when they were giving things a second try, Mason had been loath to have Scarlet adopt Luna right away. He could always do it himself, then have Scarlet do it down the road when Luna was a little older. All it changed, really, was the name on the birth certificate, nothing more. Luna wouldn't love Scarlet any less and vice versa. Given the discussions she'd had with her attorneys, it made sense to wait.

But now he knew he couldn't.

Mason had never been able to give her the biological child she wanted. He hadn't been able to do what was necessary to keep their adopted son. He'd basically taken Luna from her the same way. But he could fix this. He could offer Scarlet the chance to adopt Luna now. That way, neither of them could take the child from the other. Scarlet could feel secure. Mason would know that if they stayed married, it wasn't just to keep Luna in her life, and Scarlet would know that he wasn't just keeping Scarlet around because he was afraid to parent on his own.

It was perfect.

Flipping through the pages, he found the number of the family attorney handling the adoption. It took a few minutes for him to explain what he wanted. Since his lawyer was aware of the separation, he knew it was an odd request, but he was adamant about it. In the worst-case scenario, Luna would still have two parents who loved her, and that was the most important part. That was what he'd promised Jay.

The updated paperwork would be ready tomorrow for him to pick up. Once he had it in hand, he would go straight to the beach house. Hopefully, in the next twenty-four hours, he would figure out just what to say when he got there.

Mason hung up the phone and merrily took the stairs two at a time until he very nearly collided with Carroll at the bottom. "Sorry about that," he said, flattening against the wall out of her way.

Carroll looked at him suspiciously. "Are you okay, Mr. Spencer? You seem different. At least, different since we've moved out here."

"Well, I'm trying to work on something that might change everything." Mason didn't want to tell the nanny too much and get her hopes up. Of course, she might abandon him to go live with Scarlet and Luna if given the choice. He hadn't been the best boss or roommate lately as he skulked around the house.

"Well, I hope what you're working on is a big, fat apology to Mrs. Spencer so she takes you back."

Mason couldn't help being curious about her response. "Why is that?"

She looked around the house and held her arms out. "It's a perfectly nice house in a good neighborhood. I'm sure you paid a fortune for it. But I don't like it here. Luna doesn't like it here. I daresay that you don't even like it here. I don't know what happened between you and Mrs. Spencer, but I hope that whatever has you smiling all of a sudden is going to fix this mess and we'll get to move home."

Mason grinned and patted her on the shoulder. "I hope so, too, Carroll. I hope so, too."

Twelve

Scarlet was going stir-crazy.

It had been two weeks without a word from Mason. Surely by now he'd filed the divorce papers, but not even her attorney had called. She was going to go insane from the deafening silence of the empty house.

She'd tried to get away from it. Despite April's protests, she'd gone into the office every day. Her work there wasn't impacted by her broken heart. That was at the core of her creativity. Until she was healed, the brushes were useless. She might as well work on spreadsheets and inventory so she could be productive in her grief.

It was Sunday, however. April told her that if she showed up today, she would change the alarm codes on her and all the alarms would go off when she tried to get in. That threat, albeit hollow, was enough to keep her home today, at least. She didn't really want to deal with the police and explain to them why her own employee had basically locked her out of her building.

Scarlet settled for sitting on the deck, watching the ocean. The roar of the waves was a soothing white noise that allowed her to simply disengage. That was the best she could hope for at this point. Eventually, she would pick up and move on, but not yet. She was allowing herself the grace to get through this in her own time so she could heal. If she could heal.

The sound of the doorbell echoed from inside the house. Scarlet frowned as she got up from her chair. She wasn't expecting company.

She whipped open the front door and froze in

place when she saw Mason standing on her welcome mat. He was wearing his favorite blue jeans and his worn brown leather jacket he'd had since they started dating. She blinked her eyes twice to make sure he was real and not her imagination conjuring the Mason of her past. He was still there. Scarlet bit at her lip, unsure what to do now. She hadn't been prepared for this at all, and it probably showed.

"Hello, Scarlet."

Mason gave her a soft smile that threatened to undermine her resolve to stay strong. She wasn't sure why he was here, but she knew she shouldn't get her hopes up. He probably forgot his laptop charger or something and had to stop by and pick it up. He didn't even have the courtesy to bring the baby with him for the visit. Maybe that was for the best, though. Space would help. She hoped.

"I wasn't expecting you today," Scarlet said, skipping the pleasantries. "I wasn't expecting you ever again, actually. Did you forget something at the house?"

Mason shook his head. "No, Scarlet, I just came to talk to you."

To talk? "About what?" she asked.

He looked around the front stoop awkwardly and shuffled on his feet. "Can I come in?"

As much as she knew she shouldn't, Scarlet was desperate for someone to be in the house other than herself. Without replying, she took a step backward and allowed him to enter.

He brushed past her as he stepped into the house, smelling like leather and his favorite cologne. She tried not to breathe it in but had to draw in a breath before she turned blue. "What can I do for you today?" she asked as she casually led him to the couches in the living room. She thought about offering him a beverage but decided she was being hospitable enough as it was.

She sat down in a chair, forcing him into the couch across from her. Mason settled into his seat looking as uncomfortable as she felt. "Luna is doing well," he offered. "I think she misses you."

Scarlet gritted her teeth together. It was bad enough that she was miserable; she didn't want to know that Luna missed her. She'd already lost too many people in her young life.

"I miss you, too, Scarlet."

She froze in place, her breath held captive in her lungs. She didn't know what to say. Was it better to be honest and admit she missed him as well, or to be stoic and let him think she was over him? "Divorce is hard," she said, opting for another tactic: avoidance.

Scarlet watched as his blue eyes searched her face for something. He hunched over in his seat, gripping his hands together between his knees. He appeared to be considering his options. She wasn't sure what those options could be, or why he was even here, telling her these things. Could he really be missing her? Could he be here trying to reconcile and she was stonewalling him?

"I miss you, too," she added quickly.

A bit of hope appeared in Mason's eyes, but it didn't make it to his smile. "The other day, when you signed the divorce papers, I didn't know what to do. I didn't want a divorce. I was happier than I'd ever been with you and with Luna. It was the last thing I wanted."

"You didn't seem happy. You were distant and moody. You completely withdrew from everyone."

"I know. And I'm sorry. I was having trouble reconciling my happiness with my guilt over my brother losing everything. Being without you these few weeks has helped me realize that Jay would want me to be happy. He would want a loving, joyful home for Luna, and I was letting my grief ruin it for everyone."

"So, what…you want to come home?" Her brain warred with itself over what the answer would be if he said yes. Fool me twice…she didn't want to be a fool again. And yet, a part of her would always be a fool where Mason was concerned.

"Yes, I would. We all would. But before you say yes or no, I want to give you something."

Scarlet hadn't noticed anything in Mason's hands but a manila envelope. She presumed it had something divorce related in it. It certainly wasn't flowers or something like that stashed away. Not that she was a fan of flowers.

"Scarlet, when we got married seven years ago, we wrote our own vows. Do you remember?"

That was a silly question. Who forgot their wedding vows? "I do."

"And do you remember the part where I vowed to do anything to make you happy? That I'd give you the moon if that was what you wanted?"

Scarlet felt the prickle of tears in her eyes at the mention of that moment. He'd looked so handsome, his hands trembling slightly as he read his handwritten vows to her. She had no doubt in that moment that he loved her more than anything on earth and he would give her the moon if she asked for it. Young, idealistic love. "I remember. But that was a long time ago, Mason."

He shook his head. "It doesn't matter how long ago it was. It's as true today as it was seven years ago. I know what you want, Scarlet. More than anything. You want a baby. No, not a baby. You want Luna. And I'm going to do whatever it takes to make that happen."

Scarlet flinched. He couldn't be serious. "Are you offering her to me in the settlement?" she joked.

Mason smiled. "No, of course not. She's not a vacation home, she's a child. But I am offering you the chance to be her mother. Legally. Forever." He held up the envelope. "I've had the paperwork drawn up for both of us to adopt Luna. When this is finalized, you will have just as many rights to her as I do. You will be her mother in every way that counts and no one, including me, is going to take her away from you. No matter what happens with us."

Scarlet's jaw dropped open the longer he spoke. He was dead serious about this. When he was done, she held up her hand. "Wait, you're saying that you're willing to do this even if I still want the divorce? That we'll share custody of Luna no matter what?"

"Yes." He looked as serious as he had when he said *I do.*

"Why?" It was all Scarlet could say. He didn't have to do this. It wasn't her baby. She wasn't related to Luna by blood. If he was doing this, it was because he knew how much it was hurting her to lose another baby. "You don't have to do any of this."

"I'm doing it because Luna deserves a mother who loves her as much as you do. What kind of father would I be to her if I took her away from you?"

Scarlet covered her face with her hands as the tears started pouring from her. She couldn't stop them. After a moment, she felt his hand on her knee. When she opened her eyes, he was kneeling in front of her, holding a handkerchief.

"Here," he offered.

She took it, dabbing at her eyes and drying her

cheeks. "Thank you" was all she could say. For the handkerchief, for the adoption papers…for everything. "I appreciate it, even if I don't understand it."

"To be honest," Mason said, "it's not entirely selfless on my part."

"How is that?"

"Well, I don't just want a mother for Luna. I want my wife back, too."

Scarlet looked at him with puffy, red eyes, making it hard to gauge how she really felt about what he'd said. He waited a moment to let the words sink in before he continued. "I screwed up. I did the one thing you were afraid I would do. I wasn't sure how to cope with everything, so I retreated when I should've held my ground. I don't want the divorce, Scarlet."

She shook her head. "I don't want it either. But how do we stop it? You've already filed, haven't you?"

"Nope. I actually never even signed the papers."

Scarlet sat back in her seat, stunned. "You didn't? I thought for sure after I signed and you moved out that you would've pressed forward with the process."

"You'd think so. But I couldn't. They're sitting on my desk just as you left them, as I flip-flopped back and forth on what to do. I rationalized, as I did before, that you might be happier with another man who can give you everything you want. I know that I can't give you the family you hoped for. Luna is the only child I will ever have. But I'm willing to share her with you, no matter what. That's why I wanted to tell you about the adoption first. I didn't want you to say yes to taking me back just because of Luna. You will have her in your life. I want you to want me because you truly want me as I am. I just hope that I'm enough for you."

Scarlet covered his hand with hers. "You've always been enough. I just couldn't convince you of that."

Mason sat back on his heels. "You really mean that? You'd be happy just you and me and Luna?"

Scarlet nodded. "Absolutely. I know you might find this hard to believe, Mason, but I love you. Even when I signed the divorce papers, I loved you. I was just trying to make the smart choice for me."

Mason's excitement dulled. "What do you mean?"

"We've talked about this before, Mason. You run. I told you how hard it was on me the last time and you did it anyway. I knew it was coming, and that's why I tried to push you away. I was trying to protect myself and make our breakup my decision this time. But it didn't make any difference in the end. You were still gone and I still felt horrible."

"And now?" His heart stilled in his chest as he waited for her answer. Just because she loved him didn't mean she would take him back. Perhaps he'd screwed up too much. He would understand if she was afraid to trust her heart to him again. He wasn't sure he'd believe himself if he promised not to run again.

"And now, I still worry, to be honest. If we're going to raise a child together especially, I need to know I can count on you to be there, Mason. Bad things are going to happen. I can guarantee it. You need to learn a better way to cope with disappointment and pain. I need you to turn to me instead of running away from me. I need you to tell me when you're feeling overwhelmed so we can work through it together like a couple should."

Mason heard her words and he understood. His parents had never been much of a team. His father handled the office and his mother managed the home. Mason had tried to do both and got overwhelmed when it didn't work out perfectly. "You're right. I just have this feeling like I have to do it all on my own. But that's not what a marriage is about, is it?"

Scarlet shook her head. "If we're going to do this, we have to both promise to do it together. You and me and Luna against the world. Can you promise me that?"

"I'll promise you that and more. I promise I'll love you more than any man has ever loved a woman. I promise that I'll do anything to make you happy. All you have to do is ask. Remember, I promised you the moon and I'll find a way to climb up there and snatch it from the sky if you asked."

"And if you start to feel overwhelmed or stressed?" she pressed.

"I'll talk to you about it. Maybe I'll try a fishing trip in Tahoe or something to clear my head the next time. But I promise to always come home to you. I mean that."

Scarlet's dark eyes surveyed his face for a moment before her lips softened into a smile. "I love you," she said before lunging out of her chair and into his arms.

Mason straightened up to catch her. He wrapped

his arms around her waist and buried his face in her neck. The scent of her shampoo was like a welcome home, a reminder that the familiar was once again in his grasp. "I love you, too," he whispered into her ear. "More than you will ever know."

Scarlet pulled away to look down at him. She cradled his face in her hands. "I know." Then she leaned down to give him a kiss. Her lips were soft and hesitant at first, almost embodying how she felt about everything between them. It didn't take long, however, for her to give in to the kiss and leave her reservations behind.

It felt amazing to hold Scarlet, and know that this time he was never going to let her go. She was his, for always. He relished every moment of their embrace after going two long weeks without touching her. He wanted to hold her in his arms and kiss her until they were both out of breath, but he knew they had other things to attend to. They could pick up where they left off tonight. And every night from here on out.

Finally, reluctantly, he pulled away. Mason stood, taking Scarlet's hands and pulling her up from her chair with him. Every step they took from here was on the path of their new life together. He couldn't wait to see what was in store for them.

"Let's call Carroll and tell her the good news. I'm sure she'll immediately start packing to come home."

He laughed. "We will, but we have something we need to do first."

Scarlet looked up at him with confusion. "What?"

Mason held up the envelope in his hand. "We have to sign the adoption papers and drop them off at the attorney's office. It takes forever to process them and get them in front of the judge as it is." He took her by the hand and led her over to the dining room table. He opened up the envelope, flipping through the legal pages until he reached the one where they both had to sign. He held out a pen to her. "You first."

She took it from him, her hand trembling with excitement or nerves, he wasn't sure which. Gripping the pen, she signed the page, and unlike when she signed the divorce papers, her name was written in her neat cursive penmanship. When she was finished, she handed him the pen and he did the same.

When he was done signing, he slipped the pages back inside and capped the pen. Turning to look at Scarlet, he noticed she had tears shimmering in her dark eyes. "What's the matter?" He wasn't expecting her to cry at a moment like this. Excitement, joy, sure, but not tears.

"Do you realize that you've fulfilled your promise from the day we married?"

Mason's brow furrowed. "To love, honor and cherish you until death?"

"No. You said you'd do anything for me and you did that with Luna. You've given me the moon."

Epilogue

Scarlet didn't recognize the number when the phone rang that afternoon. She was in the midst of preparations for Luna's second-birthday celebration. The deck had been transformed into a pink extravaganza. Caterers were setting up the food, the cake had been delivered moments ago and guests would be arriving within the hour. Any other day she might've been able to identify the number of their adoption attorney's office.

"Hello?" she said.

"Hello, Scarlet? This is Peter Vann. Do you have a moment?"

"Of course. Is something wrong?" Scarlet tried not to let her concern be evident in her voice. She settled down at the dining room table, expecting bad news. *Not today*, she prayed. Not on her baby's birthday.

Luna's adoption had been finalized months ago, but the way things had ended with Evan taught her that nothing was ever final in that regard. Perhaps one of Rachel's relatives had come forward to fight for the baby—and more likely, the sizable estate that came along with her.

"No, nothing is wrong. I'm actually calling because I have some good news you and Mason might be interested to hear. I just received a call from child services."

Good news from child services? "Yes?" she pressed.

"It seems they have taken a little boy into custody and they're looking for a home to place him in. The mother has terminated her rights, so he's eligible to be adopted. They contacted us directly because they thought you and Mason might be interested in him."

She winced at his words, torn between the fantasy and reality of what this could mean for their family. Both she and Mason were content in just having Luna. "I don't know, Peter. I told you before that Luna was the exception. I don't think either of us are willing to chance another adoption scenario after what happened before. It's too risky."

Peter chuckled. "I think you'll be very interested in this one. He's two and a half years old, brown hair, brown eyes, in good health, and his name...is Evan."

Scarlet's heart skipped a beat. She couldn't believe she'd heard the attorney correctly. "Evan? Our Evan?"

"The very same. If you want him back, he's yours, Scarlet. They reviewed his history and wanted to give you two the first chance to adopt him before he gets placed elsewhere."

She could barely focus on his words as Peter continued to talk. All she needed to know was that her baby boy was coming back to her. Scarlet stood up and placed the phone against her chest to muffle her voice as she shouted, "Mason! Come quick! Evan is coming home."

* * * * *

MILLS & BOON®
Hardback – August 2017

ROMANCE

An Heir Made in the Marriage Bed	Anne Mather
The Prince's Stolen Virgin	Maisey Yates
Protecting His Defiant Innocent	Michelle Smart
Pregnant at Acosta's Demand	Maya Blake
The Secret He Must Claim	Chantelle Shaw
Carrying the Spaniard's Child	Jennie Lucas
A Ring for the Greek's Baby	Melanie Milburne
Bought for the Billionaire's Revenge	Clare Connelly
The Runaway Bride and the Billionaire	Kate Hardy
The Boss's Fake Fiancée	Susan Meier
The Millionaire's Redemption	Therese Beharrie
Captivated by the Enigmatic Tycoon	Bella Bucannon
Tempted by the Bridesmaid	Annie O'Neil
Claiming His Pregnant Princess	Annie O'Neil
A Miracle for the Baby Doctor	Meredith Webber
Stolen Kisses with Her Boss	Susan Carlisle
Encounter with a Commanding Officer	Charlotte Hawkes
Rebel Doc on Her Doorstep	Lucy Ryder
The CEO's Nanny Affair	Joss Wood
Tempted by the Wrong Twin	Rachel Bailey

MILLS & BOON®
Large Print – August 2017

ROMANCE

The Italian's One-Night Baby	Lynne Graham
The Desert King's Captive Bride	Annie West
Once a Moretti Wife	Michelle Smart
The Boss's Nine-Month Negotiation	Maya Blake
The Secret Heir of Alazar	Kate Hewitt
Crowned for the Drakon Legacy	Tara Pammi
His Mistress with Two Secrets	Dani Collins
Stranded with the Secret Billionaire	Marion Lennox
Reunited by a Baby Bombshell	Barbara Hannay
The Spanish Tycoon's Takeover	Michelle Douglas
Miss Prim and the Maverick Millionaire	Nina Singh

HISTORICAL

Claiming His Desert Princess	Marguerite Kaye
Bound by Their Secret Passion	Diane Gaston
The Wallflower Duchess	Liz Tyner
Captive of the Viking	Juliet Landon
The Spaniard's Innocent Maiden	Greta Gilbert

MEDICAL

Their Meant-to-Be Baby	Caroline Anderson
A Mummy for His Baby	Molly Evans
Rafael's One Night Bombshell	Tina Beckett
Dante's Shock Proposal	Amalie Berlin
A Forever Family for the Army Doc	Meredith Webber
The Nurse and the Single Dad	Dianne Drake

0717 GEN STD LP

MILLS & BOON®
Hardback – September 2017

ROMANCE

The Tycoon's Outrageous Proposal	Miranda Lee
Cipriani's Innocent Captive	Cathy Williams
Claiming His One-Night Baby	Michelle Smart
At the Ruthless Billionaire's Command	Carole Mortimer
Engaged for Her Enemy's Heir	Kate Hewitt
His Drakon Runaway Bride	Tara Pammi
The Throne He Must Take	Chantelle Shaw
The Italian's Virgin Acquisition	Michelle Conder
A Proposal from the Crown Prince	Jessica Gilmore
Sarah and the Secret Sheikh	Michelle Douglas
Conveniently Engaged to the Boss	Ellie Darkins
Her New York Billionaire	Andrea Bolter
The Doctor's Forbidden Temptation	Tina Beckett
From Passion to Pregnancy	Tina Beckett
The Midwife's Longed-For Baby	Caroline Anderson
One Night That Changed Her Life	Emily Forbes
The Prince's Cinderella Bride	Amalie Berlin
Bride for the Single Dad	Jennifer Taylor
A Family for the Billionaire	Dani Wade
Taking Home the Tycoon	Catherine Mann

0817 GEN STD HB

MILLS & BOON®
Large Print – September 2017

ROMANCE

The Sheikh's Bought Wife	Sharon Kendrick
The Innocent's Shameful Secret	Sara Craven
The Magnate's Tempestuous Marriage	Miranda Lee
The Forced Bride of Alazar	Kate Hewitt
Bound by the Sultan's Baby	Carol Marinelli
Blackmailed Down the Aisle	Louise Fuller
Di Marcello's Secret Son	Rachael Thomas
Conveniently Wed to the Greek	Kandy Shepherd
His Shy Cinderella	Kate Hardy
Falling for the Rebel Princess	Ellie Darkins
Claimed by the Wealthy Magnate	Nina Milne

HISTORICAL

The Secret Marriage Pact	Georgie Lee
A Warriner to Protect Her	Virginia Heath
Claiming His Defiant Miss	Bronwyn Scott
Rumours at Court (Rumors at Court)	Blythe Gifford
The Duke's Unexpected Bride	Lara Temple

MEDICAL

Their Secret Royal Baby	Carol Marinelli
Her Hot Highland Doc	Annie O'Neil
His Pregnant Royal Bride	Amy Ruttan
Baby Surprise for the Doctor Prince	Robin Gianna
Resisting Her Army Doc Rival	Sue MacKay
A Month to Marry the Midwife	Fiona McArthur

0817 GEN STD LP